RUN FOR IT

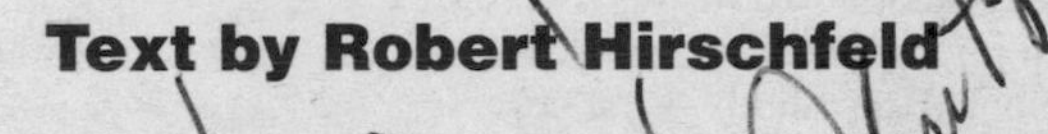

Text by Robert Hirschfeld

Little, Brown and Company
Boston New York London

First Paperback Edition

Text by Robert Hirschfeld

Library of Congress Cataloging-in-Publication Data

Hirschfeld, Robert.
Run for it : the #1 sports series for kids / Matt Christopher ; text by Robert Hirschfeld. — 1st ed.
p. cm.
Summary: Thirteen-year-old Theo, overweight and out of shape, finds that with his friend's support he just might be able to run in the race to raise money to help cancer patients like his aunt.
ISBN 0-316-34899-6 (hc) / ISBN 0-316-34914-3 (pb)
[1. Physical fitness — Fiction. 2. Perseverance (Ethics) — Fiction. 3. Running — Fiction.] I. Christopher, Matt. II. Title.
PZ7.H59794 Ru 2002
[Fic] — dc21 2001038663

10 9 8 7 6 5 4 3 2 1

COM-MO

Printed in the United States of America

1

Theo Gordimer slowly clomped up the steps to the front door of his house. His heavy backpack made his shoulders ache. His face was hot and sweaty. He shoved his blond hair out of his eyes and went inside. All he wanted to do was go to his room, dump the pack, and settle down with a video game.

Not that that would cheer him up much, but it might make him feel a little less depressed.

He heard his mother calling from the kitchen. "Theo? Is that you?"

"Yeah, Mom," he muttered as he started up the stairs to his room. By the time he reached the top step, he was puffing a little. *Great,* he thought. *One flight of stairs and I'm wiped out. What a total wimp I am.*

Theo shrugged himself out of the backpack. It

thumped onto the floor by his bed. He left it lying there and looked through his rack of video games. But nothing he saw drew his interest. Would anything brighten his mood?

Video games didn't seem to do the job. The school year was almost over and summer vacation was only three days away. Not even that fact raised his spirits. Theo sighed and sat on the edge of his bed. The springs gave out a loud squeak, as if they were complaining about his weight. Staring out the window, Theo thought about his day and when it had turned bad.

It had happened in gym class, when Mr. Breen told the boys that they were going to run a lap around the school's quarter-mile track. Now, even if Theo wasn't on the heavy side — which, to face facts, he was — he would never have picked running as a fun thing to do. It made you out of breath and tired. TV, movies, and video games — they were what he thought of as fun. But today, like it or not, Theo had to run.

He was sure he'd run more than a quarter mile in his thirteen years — just not all at once. He didn't know if he could.

"What if I can't do it?" he whispered to his best friend, Paul Baskin, as they waited for their turn.

Paul stared at Theo. "Come on! A quarter mile? You can run that far, can't you?"

Theo shook his head. "I don't know. I never have."

"Well . . . just take it easy. I bet you make it. It's no big deal."

Maybe it wasn't a big deal for Paul, who was into sports. But for Theo, a quarter of a mile seemed like a *huge* deal. Still, maybe Paul was right. He might do it.

He didn't. Halfway around the big oval track, he was gasping and feeling awful. He slowed down from what hadn't been a fast pace to begin with and started walking. Other kids passed him and a couple of them made nasty remarks as they went by.

"Yo, blubber-boy! Want a lift?"

"Move it, lardo!"

Theo wished he could disappear. After walking for a little, he managed to speed up to a sort of trot and finally staggered to the end of the lap. Mr. Breen shook his head.

"Gordimer, better lay off the doughnuts and ice cream. You need to shape up."

Theo sighed and closed his eyes. Mr. Breen was right, he guessed. He *did* need to shape up. But it seemed like such a huge job, and he didn't know how. His mom and dad wished that he'd spend less time in front of a TV and more time throwing a ball or swimming or something. They didn't get on his case about it much, but he knew how they felt. When he let himself think about it, he felt sad, even ashamed.

But, bad as this was, it wasn't the worst thing in Theo's life. The worst thing was what was happening to his aunt Marj.

Theo loved Aunt Marj, his mom's younger sister. She was great to spend time with and could always make him laugh. Aunt Marj was a cheerful, funny, lively woman who never ran out of energy. Or she *had* been, until she'd gotten sick.

Some months earlier, Marj had been told she had cancer. Since then, she'd been in and out of the hospital, getting radiation therapy and chemotherapy, which were supposed to make her better. They didn't seem to be working, not as far as Theo could see. She'd become thin and pale and spent almost all of her time in bed. Theo had gone to see her but was only allowed to stay for a few minutes. Marj was barely able to talk.

Theo had never faced such a terrible and sudden change, and it scared him. He couldn't help wondering if she was going to die. He didn't want to talk about Marj with his parents; his mother was upset enough.

Theo felt helpless, wishing there was something he could do for Marj. But there wasn't. Sure, he could visit her once in a while or phone her. But that was about it.

There was a tap on the bedroom door. Mrs. Gordimer peeked in at him. "Sweetie, are you all right? You look kind of down."

So do you, Theo thought. But all he said was, "Yeah, I'm okay. Just a little tired."

"Paul is here. Can he come up?"

"Sure." Theo sat up and swung his legs off the bed as Mrs. Gordimer left the room. He didn't feel like having company, but he didn't want to worry his mother by saying so.

Paul came in a minute later carrying his baseball glove. "Hey, Gee, let's go to the park. A bunch of guys are going to play some ball."

Theo shook his head. "I don't feel like it today. Another time, okay?"

"You sure?" Paul asked, giving Theo a curious look. "It's a good day for it."

"Yeah, well . . ." Theo stopped there. Paul looked at Theo, who looked away.

Finally, Paul said, "What's going on? Did that stuff in gym class today get to you?"

"No . . . well, yeah. But it's not just that."

"Well, what? Anything I can do?" Paul sat in Theo's desk chair.

Theo lay back on the bed. "There's nothing anyone can do."

"Hey, at least give me a clue. I mean, I'm your friend, right?"

"It's my aunt Marj. She's real sick."

"Yeah, I heard," said Paul. "I met her, she's a cool lady. How bad is it?"

"Real bad. She's been getting this treatment, but she looks terrible. And there's nothing I can do to help. I feel really bad."

"Sure. I'd feel the same way," agreed Paul. "But maybe she'll get better."

"She sure doesn't look like she's getting better." Theo felt tears blurring his eyes. "Last time I saw her, she looked awful."

Paul stood up suddenly. "You know what, Gee? I just remembered. There *is* something you could do for her. Well, sort of. If you want to give it a shot, that is."

Theo stared hopefully at his friend. "Yeah? What?"

Paul said, "You know my dad is really into running, and he hears about all these races. He found out about a five-K race that's open to all ages, and it's supposed to raise money for cancer research and help people learn about new medicines and stuff."

Theo blinked. "That sounds neat, but what does it have to do with me?"

"You could run the race. It's in three months. That would be a way to —"

Theo's loud laugh interrupted Paul. *"Me?"*

"Sure," Paul replied. "Why not?"

Theo shook his head. "After my 'run' today? Get real! By the way, what's 'five K'?"

"It means five kilometers. That's a little over three miles, which —"

"Three *miles?* I almost passed out trying to run a *quarter* of a mile! You're kidding, right?"

"No, I think you could do it," said Paul. "I'm working out to be ready for football in the fall, and I run a lot. I really like it. I bet you would, too, if you gave it a try."

Theo rolled his eyes. "Sure, you like it. *You're* an athlete. But *me?*"

Paul sighed. "You may be more athletic than you think, but unless you try, you'll never know. Anyway, it's a no on softball, huh?"

"Not today," Theo said. "I've embarrassed myself enough for one afternoon. I'll walk you down, and that'll be enough of a workout for me."

When the boys reached the front door, Paul turned to Theo. "You should talk to my dad. He could tell you how to get started in running. It doesn't have to be torture."

"Yeah, right," Theo said.

Paul looked a little irritated. "Can you just keep an open mind about it?"

"About what?" asked Mrs. Gordimer, who had heard the last part of the conversation.

Paul said, "I was telling Theo about this road race for cancer research and saying he should run in it."

Mrs. Gordimer smiled. "That sounds like a wonderful idea! Theo, you know how Marj has been trying to persuade you to get more involved in sports. She'd *love* it if you tried something like this."

"Mom," Theo said, wishing Paul had kept his mouth shut, "it's more than *three miles.* I couldn't do that. I'm not a runner."

"You *could* be a runner," Paul insisted.

Mrs. Gordimer said, "I think Paul's right, sweetie. You can at least think about it, can't you?"

Feeling trapped, Theo said, "Okay, sure, I'll think about it."

"Great!" Paul said, ignoring Theo's glare. "See you tomorrow." He ran down the front steps.

Theo's mother ruffled his hair. "Will you think about it? I wish you would."

Theo nodded. "Sure, Mom. I really will. Okay?"

Then he headed back to his room to find a video game, hoping that the subject of running would disappear and never be brought up again.

2

Theo did manage to avoid the subject of running — for two whole days. On the third day, the last day of the school year, Paul came up to him in the corridor.

"My family's having a cookout tonight to celebrate the beginning of summer vacation. Burgers, hot dogs, and ribs. Want to come?"

"Sure!" said Theo, who could almost taste all those goodies right then.

"Great!" Paul replied. "And my dad wants to talk to you about how to start a running program. We can do that before we eat."

Uh oh. Theo felt pretty sure that Paul had deliberately mentioned the food first, so that he would accept the invitation. Only after he'd accepted had Paul brought up running. Now Theo was caught.

Theo's face must have shown how he felt about

running, because Paul laughed. "Listen, all I'm asking you to do is listen to him, all right? You won't have to run if you decide not to. Just hear him out. That shouldn't take much energy. And then there'll be all those excellent goodies. It's not like I trapped you into going to the dentist."

Theo finally agreed to listen to Mr. Baskin, if only to get Paul to stop talking about it. After all, Paul was right. Listening wouldn't cost him anything, and Theo wouldn't have to do anything he didn't want to do.

Later that afternoon, Theo told his parents that he was going to the Baskins' cookout and added that Mr. Baskin was going to talk to him about running.

His parents exchanged a look. Mr. Gordimer said, "Really? Sounds interesting. Are you thinking of doing some running, son?"

His dad was trying to make it sound casual, as if it didn't matter at all whether Theo started doing something athletic. But Theo knew how his parents felt.

He shrugged. "Well, I guess I'll see what Mr. Baskin says and then decide."

"That makes sense," his dad agreed. "Anyway, the cookout sounds like fun."

When he got to the Baskins' house, Theo knew

from the delicious smells that the food was already on the grill. If he had to listen to talk about running to get some of that food, it was worth it.

Theo went around to the backyard. Mr. Baskin, a tall, slender man, was standing over his gas grill, turning some burgers. He smiled and waved to Theo.

"Hey, come on in! I understand you might be interested in running."

Even though Theo didn't think that this was an accurate description of his attitude, he said, "I appreciate you talking to me about it."

Mr. Baskin nodded. "We'll talk after we eat, if that's all right. Everybody's hungry."

The later the better, thought Theo. Paul came out the back door. "Yo, Gee! Ready to eat?"

"Always," Theo replied, grinning.

The food was great. Theo managed to gobble a hamburger, a hot dog, a bunch of ribs, some fantastic potato salad, and a couple of glasses of soda.

As Mrs. Baskin dished out ice cream, Mr. Baskin said, "Ready to talk, Theo?"

"Sure," answered Theo, hoping he sounded more eager than he felt.

"Just a minute," Paul's dad said. "I want to get

something." He went inside as Mrs. Baskin handed Theo a bowl of ice cream.

Theo dug right in. "Thanks, Mrs. B."

A minute later, Mr. Baskin returned, carrying a large leather-bound photo album. "Before we talk, I wanted you to have a look at some old pictures. Paul gave me the idea that you had some doubts about getting into running."

Theo wasn't sure what to say. "Well . . . ," he began.

Paul's dad held up a hand. "I imagine you may have been thinking, 'Oh, sure, it's fine for Paul and his father to run. They're natural athletes, they're thin. But *me* . . . I don't think so.'"

Theo was a little startled, because that was pretty much exactly what was on his mind. He smiled and said, "Uh, yeah, I guess."

Mr. Baskin sat down next to Theo, opened the album, and began leafing through it. "Sure. That's why I want you to look at some old family snapshots." He found what he was looking for and handed it to Theo. "These are pictures of me when I was your age."

Theo stared at the old photos. No doubt about it, they were of Mr. Baskin as a boy.

And, as a boy, Mr. Baskin had been *fat!* It looked

like he'd weighed even more than Theo did now. His face had been round, and he'd had a double chin.

"Wow," Theo whispered, looking up at Mr. Baskin.

Paul's dad grinned. "Yeah, wow. That was me when I was thirteen. Surprised?"

"Yeah! I mean, I just figured that you were always, you know . . ."

"That I'd always been skinny," Mr. Baskin finished for him. "Well, I wasn't. Far from it, as you can see. I was heavy until I turned fourteen, when I got into running."

Theo was still trying to absorb the notion of a pudgy Mr. Baskin. "How come? What made you decide to change?"

Mr. Baskin smiled. "Not *what* — it was more a matter of *who.* A girl named Charlene Kramer, with big, blue eyes and dimples made me change. I was crazy about her.

"I figured, no way a cute girl like Charlene would pay attention to me unless I did something about how I looked. Maybe I was wrong to think that, but I did. Then and there, I made up my mind to do something about it."

"So you started running," said Theo.

"That's right," Mr. Baskin said. He looked at the photos of himself and shook his head. "Funny thing is, even after I lost weight, Charlene never did pay attention to me. But I've been running ever since. If I ever see Charlene again, I'll thank her. She changed my life for the better, and she never even knew it."

"And you really found you liked running?" Theo asked.

"Yes! It took me maybe three weeks. One day I discovered that I was enjoying myself. And I still do."

He closed the album. "Let me make my pitch about what you can get out of running. Number one, I think you'll like it, like I did."

"And like I'm doing now," added Paul.

"Number two, if you do this regularly, you'll lose weight — like I did. It's simple. Think of the food you eat as fuel. If you take in more fuel than you burn in activity, you have to store what you don't use. Your body stores it as fat. If you burn up more fuel than you take in, your body burns up fat to make up the difference.

"And, number three, you may become more interested in other sports and do better in them. You'll also feel better about yourself, which is probably the best thing of all."

Theo felt a sudden surge of hope. "Mr. Baskin, this five-K race is in about three months. You think I could be ready for that?"

Mr. Baskin studied Theo for a moment. "Could you run a five-K race in three months? I think you could enter and probably finish it. That isn't to say that you'd *win.* But you could be running that distance in three months, yes."

Theo felt excited by the thought. He could imagine how Aunt Marj would react if she knew he was going to do this for her. If there was a chance he could really do it . . .

"I'd like to try," he said suddenly. "I mean, that'd be great, if I could run that race."

"I'll be happy to help get you started," Mr. Baskin said. "Whether you stick with it is up to you. You have to make a serious commitment to running. Are you willing to do that?"

Theo was surprised to find himself saying, "I think so. When can I start?"

"Tomorrow is Saturday," said Paul's father. "I can

meet you in the park tomorrow morning, if that works for you."

Theo grinned. "Yeah, that'd be great! I really appreciate this, Mr. Baskin."

The man replied, "No problem. You remind me of me at your age. How does eleven o'clock sound?"

"Okay," Theo replied. "Uh, do I need any equipment? Anything special?"

"For tomorrow," said Mr. Baskin, "you need a pair of sneakers, comfortable clothes to work out in, and a wristwatch."

"I'd like to come, too," said Paul, "if it's all right with Theo."

"Sure," Theo said. It was hard to believe. But he was going to do it! After all, what did he have to lose? Except maybe some fat?

3

Dressed in shorts, a T-shirt, and sneakers and wearing an old wristwatch of his father's, Theo walked to the park the next morning. It was a warm, sunny day, and he passed a number of runners of different ages. He thought that soon he might be one of them.

His parents had been delighted when Theo told them of his plan. They suggested that he telephone Aunt Marj. Theo had hesitated, reluctant to disappoint her if he didn't meet his goal. But the temptation had proved too strong.

Marj had sounded weak on the phone, but there was no mistaking the pleasure she had felt. "That's wonderful news, hon. It's the best medicine I could have!"

"I might not be able to do it," Theo had cautioned her.

"I'll bet you will. And just knowing that you care enough to try is wonderful. Good luck, hon, and let me know how it's going."

Theo caught sight of Paul and Mr. Baskin waiting near a path under some trees. He waved to them, and they waved back.

"Hi, Theo," Mr. Baskin said. "You ready?"

"I guess," Theo said. "So, do we just, like, start running?"

"Not yet," said Paul's dad. "The first thing we begin with is stretching. You're going to begin and end every workout by doing some stretches. They'll protect you from injuries like pulled muscles."

Mr. Baskin went over to a nearby building and said, "First, I'll do each stretch, and then you do it. This one is for your calf muscles."

Mr. Baskin stood a few feet from the wall and stepped forward on his right foot. He leaned forward and rested his forearms against the wall so that his left leg was straight and the heel of his left foot was off the ground.

He looked back to Theo. "Now I'm going to push against the wall and, at the same time, press my left heel down toward the ground — not too hard, *gently* — to stretch the left calf muscle. Then I'll hold that position while I count slowly to ten."

After this, Mr. Baskin switched legs and stretched the calf of his right leg. Then he gestured to Theo. "Let's see you try it."

Theo got into position and pushed down with his left heel.

"Careful, not too hard," cautioned Paul's father. "Can you feel the stretch?"

"Yeah," Theo said.

"Hold it for a ten count, then switch legs," Mr. Baskin said.

After Theo had finished, Mr. Baskin said, "Okay. Paul, your turn."

Once his son had finished, Mr. Baskin said, "Now for the thigh muscles."

Theo learned ten stretches in all, for his legs, arms, and back. When they were finished, he said, "I don't think I can remember all this."

"Don't worry," Mr. Baskin replied. "I have pictures and instructions for everything in the car. When we're finished, I'll give them to you. Once you've been doing this awhile, you won't need the instructions, you'll have it all memorized."

"Okay," said Theo.

"Once you've been working out for a while, you'll be more flexible, and then you may want to repeat each stretch two or three times instead of just once."

Theo nodded. "So, now do we run?"

Mr. Baskin shook his head. "Not right away. First, we're going to walk."

Theo was startled. "Walk?"

"You don't want to try to do too much all at once," said Paul.

"Right," his father agreed. "So first, we're going to walk for ten minutes. Then, we'll run a little. Ready?"

Theo nodded and the three set off, fairly fast, but not fast enough to exhaust Theo. As they walked, Mr. Baskin explained the schedule he wanted Theo to use.

"What you're doing today is the pattern for your first week. You walk the first ten minutes. For the second ten minutes, you'll run until you have to slow down. Then you'll walk for a minute and start running again, and so on, until the second ten minutes is over. Finally, you'll walk for ten minutes more, do your stretches, and that's it."

"That's all?" Theo was relieved. "That doesn't sound too bad."

"It isn't too bad," Paul said. "You see? I *told* you."

"The idea is to build yourself up, a little at a time," explained Mr. Baskin. "During the next eight weeks, you'll do more and more running and less walking. Also, the walking you do will be faster. The idea is to build up your endurance without exhausting you.

"Little by little, you build up your muscles, including your heart. At the same time, you build up your oxygen intake, which will give you more energy. You'll start to feel a difference — not right away, but pretty soon."

"And you think I'll be able to run three miles in three months?" Theo asked.

"I think so," answered Paul's dad. "Along with the stretching instructions, I'll give you a timetable to use. Every week for the next eight weeks, you'll increase your running time and cut down your walking time."

Mr. Baskin's watch suddenly beeped. "Time to do a little running," he said. "Now remember — don't push too hard. This is only your first day."

Theo had to stop and walk three times during the ten minutes. He felt embarrassed, like he'd done a pathetic workout. As they started walking the last ten minutes, Theo muttered, "That was totally lame, huh?"

"Lighten up," Paul said. "It was your first time. You'll get better."

"Paul's right," said his father. "I think I had even more trouble my first time. Don't get down on yourself so quickly."

As they walked, Mr. Baskin began talking about running. "I love this sport. You can do it anywhere, anytime. You don't have to have a lot of expensive equipment. You can compete in races, or you can just run for the heck of it. Every time I run, I feel great afterward — like my body is full of energy. I know I'm healthier than I would be if I didn't run." He grinned. "And if I ever see Charlene Kramer, boy, will *she* be impressed."

Paul said, "I've only been doing it for a month now, but I really like it, too. Once you've worked at it a little more, we can run together."

Theo felt a little better.

Mr. Baskin's watch beeped. "Let's do those stretches."

After the three had stretched, Paul asked, "How do you feel? Ready to do it again tomorrow?"

Theo thought about it for a moment. "Yeah," he said. "I am. You were right to get me into this."

"Want a ride home?" Mr. Baskin asked, after he'd given Theo the stretching instructions and running schedule.

"No, I guess I'll walk," Theo said.

Mr. Baskin started the car. "Suit yourself. And call me if you have any questions. I'll probably check with you now and then to see how it's going."

"See you, Gee," Paul said.

Theo waved as the car moved away. He'd be back tomorrow, and he'd do the same routine.

Except maybe just a little better.

4

The following day was Sunday, and Theo worked out by himself, using Mr. Baskin's charts to help him remember the stretches. As he started out, he felt a little nervous, but soon relaxed and just got into the rhythm of moving. Without Mr. Baskin along, Theo wasn't sure how fast he was going. But he thought he might be walking a little faster than the previous day.

He wondered if it would be a good idea to do his walking and running on the school track at least once a week, so that he'd know how far he was going and at what speed. That way, he'd know how much progress he was making.

The first ten minutes went by surprisingly fast, and Theo began to run. One of the pointers Mr. Baskin had given him yesterday concerned breathing. He should keep his breathing steady and rhythmical. He focused on that. When he had to slow down to a walk, Theo was pleasantly surprised. He had run for almost three minutes! That was better than he had done the day before. He resolved to try not to walk more than one more time during the middle ten minutes today.

And he did it! Determined not to walk, Theo did have to slow down during his last run, looking at his watch every few seconds to see when the ten minutes was over. He forgot about keeping his breathing even and steady and was happy to keep breathing at all. When the second hand of the watch finally showed that he could stop, he was panting and sweating heavily.

But during the whole ten minutes, Theo had only walked for two. In other words, he had run for eight minutes. No doubt about it, he'd made progress!

As he walked the last ten minutes, Theo realized he must have had a big grin on his face, because people coming his way grinned back. But he felt good. Maybe he'd reach his goal, after all. It began to seem possible to him.

He finished the last walk and did his stretches,

feeling really great. Theo wasn't sure whether he felt great because he'd done better today or because running did that for you, like the Baskins said. But it didn't really matter. It was nice to feel so good, whatever the reason.

When he arrived at home, his father saw him come in. "How did it go?" he asked.

"Okay," Theo replied. "Actually, it was really good. I did better than yesterday."

"That's great news," said Mr. Gordimer. "Want to tell Aunt Marj? We're going to see her, and you're welcome to join us."

"Sure," Theo said. "I'll get cleaned up."

Mr. Gordimer said, "Marj just finished her last chemotherapy session, so this is sort of a congratulations visit. I don't think we'll stay for long — she's never up for long visits just after finishing one of those. But she'll be happy to hear your news."

"I'll be ready in a few minutes," Theo said as he ran up to his room.

When the Gordimers arrived at Marj's place, Marj's aide, Louise, let them in. Louise had been staying with Marj during her recovery. She was a young woman who seemed to be cheerful all the time, which, Theo figured, was a good quality to have for someone who did that kind of work. He knew that Marj had a high opinion of Louise, whose services had been vital for the last several months.

"How is she doing?" asked Theo's mother as Louise closed the front door.

Louise's usual sunny look turned a little less bright. "Well, you know how it is. Right after she gets back from the therapy, she's not real strong. But that'll pass. And she's looking forward to seeing you. Just let's keep it pretty short today, all right?"

Theo, who thought he was prepared to see his aunt looking not very well, was nevertheless shocked when they went into Marj's room. She was lying in bed, propped up on a few pillows. She seemed even thinner than when he'd seen her last, and her skin was chalky. Her hair was almost completely gone! There were only some wisps of white left.

Mrs. Gordimer bent over and kissed her sister. "Good to see you home," she said softly.

"Hi, Gordimers," Marj whispered, managing a weak smile.

"Nice to know that you're through with those

treatments," Mr. Gordimer said, sitting in a chair near the bed.

"I thought they'd never end," Marj agreed. Her eyes fell on Theo. "Hi, hon! Give your aunt a kiss!"

Theo came to the side of the bed and kissed Marj's cheek. She looked at him for a moment and must have seen something in his expression.

"It's not as bad as all that, hon. I don't believe you ever saw me just after I finished chemo. I always look like this for a couple of days. But it passes."

"Of course it does," agreed Mr. Gordimer. "You'll be up and about in no time."

Marj put a hand to her head. "It's the hair, isn't it? Chemo does that to a lot of people. But they tell me it'll grow back. And if it doesn't, well, there are always wigs. I can change my hairstyle every day if I want."

Theo remembered that the last few times he'd seen Marj, she'd been wearing a baseball cap. Now he understood why.

"I've started running," Theo said. "Today was my second day."

Marj's smile grew a little wider. "That's wonderful!"

"Well, it's only a start," Theo said. "No big deal."

"Sure, it's a big deal," said Marj. "Taking the first step is a big deal. And it makes me very pleased to know you're doing it."

Mrs. Gordimer passed along some family news to Marj, and the family chatted for a few minutes. Then, Louise came into the bedroom.

"I hate to break this up, but Marj needs to get her rest. I think it's time to say our good-byes now."

The Gordimers stood up, and each of them gave Marj a kiss and said good-bye. When Theo's turn came, Marj squeezed his hand.

"You keep this up. I want you to tell me all about it. I'm proud of you."

"You just get better," Theo said. "*I'm* proud of *you.*"

There was little talk in the car after the Gordimers left Marj's place. Theo had tried to keep up a confident appearance during the visit, but he was feeling very upset. From the way Marj looked, he wondered if she would ever recover. But there was no way that he would say any such thing within his mother's hearing.

But Theo was pretty sure that Mrs. Gordimer

shared his mood. She sat with her eyes closed, looking unhappy and on the verge of tears.

It was Mr. Gordimer who finally broke the silence. "Look, I know that was rough on all of us. But let's try not to get too discouraged, all right?"

"She looks so weak and tired," his wife said.

Mr. Gordimer kept his eyes on the road while he spoke. "Dear, she's looked terrible *every time* after the chemo. Then she slowly gets stronger. No reason to expect this time to be any different. Remember Jerry Abrams?"

"The man in your office who had cancer?" Theo asked.

"Right," said Theo's dad. "Jerry went through the same routine — radiation, chemo, the works. I visited him a couple of times and figured he would never make it. Well, guess what?

"Jerry's on the mend. He has been for two years now, and he's doing fine. Cancer isn't an automatic death sentence, not anymore — far from it."

"Really?" Theo asked. "He got better?"

"He sure did," said Mr. Gordimer. "And if anybody I know is a good candidate for complete recovery, it's Marj. She's one tough lady. She's always been healthy and active, and she's as stubborn as they come. No way will she just lie down and quit."

Mrs. Gordimer nodded. "You're right, of course, but I get so worried for her."

"Sure you do," her husband said. "But don't let it get to you. The most important thing we can do — all of us, you, too, Theo — is to think positive thoughts and be there for her. We have to let her know we're rooting for her. That can make a difference."

Theo sat back, feeling a little less gloomy. His father was right. The other thing he could do, personally, was to keep running.

5

A few days later, Theo went to his school's track to do his workout. The first ten-minute walk went well. Theo was happy to realize that he covered well over half a mile. He was certain that this was considerably more than he'd been able to do less than a week before. The big question was: how far would he be able to run nonstop?

Before starting, he quickly went over a few of Mr. Baskin's tips, especially the one about keeping his breathing steady. Then he started. Before he'd finished half of his first running lap, Theo knew that he was going to finish the whole lap without stopping . . . and then some. He was relaxed and not feeling wiped out at all. *Amazing!* he thought, as his legs kept pumping away.

He finished the first lap and kept going. Shortly

after he began his second lap, Theo began to feel a little winded, but resisted the temptation to slow to a walk just yet. As he ran, he thought about the kids who had teased him in gym class that day and smiled to himself. He wished they were there to see him now.

Well, maybe they *would* see him, soon enough. He suddenly realized that he had gone more than halfway around the track a second time! Could he do a complete half mile? He gritted his teeth. He'd sure try. His breathing got a little faster and harder as the end of the lap came into sight, but Theo knew that he was going to do it. At the end of the half mile, he slowed to a walk and looked at his watch. It had taken him just over five and a half minutes. He walked slowly at first, then faster as he got his wind back.

When the one-minute walking interval ended, Theo started running again. He didn't have to stop until it was time to start walking again.

He'd run for nine of the ten minutes and only had to walk once! He felt wonderful. He began walking again, feeling stronger and more confident with every step. He'd do it! He'd run that five-K!

This was the New Theo, and there was no telling how fast he'd get!

At the end of the final ten minutes, Theo worked out that he'd been walking at about four-and-a-half miles an hour. Hardly a world record, he knew, but better — *much* better — than the old Theo was ever able to do. Tomorrow was the last day of his first week, and Mr. Baskin's schedule called for Theo to take a day off.

Still feeling pumped, Theo phoned Paul that evening after dinner.

"Hey, Gee, how you doing?" Paul asked.

"Fantastic! I had a really good workout today! This is going great!"

"No kidding? That's really cool, Gee. My dad's going to be glad to hear it. How far did you run?"

"I ran a half mile without stopping!" Theo said. "Remember that day in gym? I couldn't make half a lap!"

Paul sounded genuinely pleased at Theo's progress. "Way to go, Gee! Hey, want to go to the park with me tomorrow and play some ball? There'll be a bunch of guys there."

Theo hesitated, out of old habit, but then said,

"Sure, why not? Sounds good. I'll come by your place. Tell your dad thanks again for me."

"Right! Oh, how's your aunt doing?" Paul asked. "Any better?"

Thinking of Marj, Theo felt his mood darken. "Well, maybe a little. She's still pretty weak. But it's going to take time, you know."

"Sure," Paul said, quickly. "But I bet she's going to be better soon. I bet she'll be able to come and watch you in that race."

"Wouldn't that be amazing?" Theo fell silent, thinking about that possibility. It might happen. There was no way to know for sure. "Well, anyway, see you tomorrow."

"Bye, Gee!"

Theo hung up the phone and closed his eyes, imagining himself running in a real race, with his parents and Marj cheering him on from the sideline. It was a very nice dream. Maybe this dream might even come true.

The next day, Theo biked over to Paul's, and the two boys rode to the park. Theo was still excited about what he'd done the day before.

In the midst of talking about what he was going to do at the track in the coming week, Theo stopped and looked at Paul.

"What are you smiling at?"

Paul shrugged. "Oh, nothing. It's just that, up until a week ago, I'd have had to drag you out onto a track. The only action you liked was what you saw on a video screen. And now . . . well, it's a huge change, that's all."

Theo nodded. "Yeah, I guess it seems pretty funny. But it's for real! And I owe it all to you. If you hadn't pushed me into trying it out, I might never have done it."

They had arrived at the ball field, where they got off their bikes and locked them. Some other boys were already at the field. Paul and Theo waved to them as they walked over.

"Anyway," Theo said as they walked, "I think maybe I'll be able to run the full ten minutes without stopping by the end of this week. Maybe we can work out together once or twice."

"Sounds cool, Gee," Paul said.

"Did I hear something about working out?" asked Van Sluman, one of the other boys waiting to play.

Van was a wiry, freckle-faced redhead who seemed to enjoy making fun of Theo more than anyone else. He'd been one of the boys who had ragged him when Theo hadn't been able to run a full lap on the school track.

Theo didn't say anything to Van, but Paul did. "Yeah, Theo's started doing some running. He's going to get into shape."

Van laughed and looked at the other grinning boys. "Get into shape? *Him?* What shape is he going to get into? A big, round ball?"

"Real funny, Sluman," Paul snapped.

Theo flushed, wishing Paul had kept his mouth shut.

Van turned to the rest of the group. "Hear that, guys? Theo's working out. He's going to be a runner." He turned back to Theo, sneering. "How far you going to run, big boy? Down to the candy store and back?"

Stung by the laughter, Theo couldn't stop himself. "I'm going to run in a race in a few months. A five-K race."

Van rolled his eyes in a look of comic disbelief. "Five K? *You're* going to run five K? Yeah, right!"

"That's more than three miles!" said one of the other kids. "They won't need a stopwatch to time you. They'll need a calendar!"

"He's going to do it," said Paul, standing up for his friend. "You'll see. He's already doing a lot better than he used to."

"Uh-huh," Van said. "A lot better. Like, he can make a hundred yards now without fainting?"

Theo swallowed and said, "I'm going to do it. I will."

Van stared hard at Theo. "Tell you what, Gordo. If you run a whole five-K race, I'll push a peanut all the way down Main Street with my nose. On my hands and knees."

Paul put a hand on Theo's shoulder. "You better start practicing with a peanut, Sluman, because he's going to run that race. And *I'm* going to make sure you do what you said you'd do."

Theo, who only a few minutes ago had felt really confident in himself, suddenly wasn't sure at all. He was back to the old Theo, wishing he hadn't gotten involved in this running stuff, doubting that he had what it took. Van was right about him, there was no way in the world he could run that far. He stood silent and miserable until Van and his buddies got bored with picking on him and chose up sides for the softball game.

As usual, Theo was the last one picked.

As his team went out to start the game — Theo was put in right field, where he'd do the least damage — Paul whispered to him, "Don't let that guy bother you. You can do it, and you're going to make him look like a total jerk."

Theo nodded and trotted to a corner of the outfield, where he stood hoping that nothing would be hit in his direction. As the game began, Theo couldn't focus on what was going on in the field. He kept thinking about what the other boys thought of him, and that they were probably right. He was what he was, and that was that.

"*Hey, Gordimer!* You sleeping out there?" The yell from a teammate jolted Theo out of his daydream to notice that a ball *had* been hit in his direction and rolled right by him. He ran after it and threw it back to the infield, but not before the hitter had made it all the way to third base.

"Yo, Gordo, if you want to take a nap, find a bed

somewhere!" yelled a second teammate. Theo looked at his feet and said nothing.

The rest of the game wasn't much better, although Theo managed not to get so distracted again. But he misplayed a couple of fly balls that he should have caught easily. When his team was at bat, he did no better. With runners at first and third and one out, Theo hit a little bouncer to shortstop that resulted in a double play to end one inning. The ground ball had been hit so slowly that only the lead-footed Theo could not have beaten out the throw to first. In another at bat, he actually struck out, something that almost never happened in the kind of slow pitch softball they played.

Even by Theo's normal standards, he played terribly. After a while, he was able to tune out all the nasty remarks of the other guys. Only Paul refused to join in the fun of teasing Theo, but after a while even Paul stopped defending him. Finally, after what seemed like many hours, the game ended.

As Theo and Paul trudged back to their bikes, Theo was too depressed to talk. Paul finally said, "You shouldn't let that kind of stuff get to you the way it does. That only makes a guy like Van keep going."

"What am I supposed to do? Get into a fight with him?" Theo demanded. "What do you mean, 'shouldn't let that kind of stuff get to me'?"

Paul bent down to unlock his bike. "Of course you shouldn't fight him. Just prove that he's wrong. Show him up."

Theo stood up from removing the chain from his bike. "How am I supposed to prove that he's wrong if he happens to be right? Because he is. I'm not an athlete, and I was dumb to pretend that I was one! Now, if I don't do this race, they'll be on my back forever about it. I should have just . . ." He didn't finish the sentence.

Paul waited a moment as they pedaled toward home. "You should have just what? You saying you're sorry you started running?!"

"I don't know!" Theo burst out. "I don't know what I should do."

"Then I'll tell you," said Paul. "You should keep it up. Then, when you run that race, they're going to look dumb. . . . And I'm going to make sure that Van pushes that peanut!"

"But I don't think I can!" Theo insisted.

Paul waved a hand in disgust. "Because Van says so? You're going to let *Van Sluman* decide what you can and can't do? Tell me, yes or no: did you make real progress this week?"

"Well, sure," admitted Theo. "But —"

"No buts. You got better. You can keep getting better, too — unless you quit."

"Sure, I ran half a mile," Theo said. "That's a long way from five kilometers."

"When you think of that day in gym class, running half a mile is a big step in the right direction," Paul said. "But you can't get discouraged — especially not because of some dumb teasing. You owe it to your aunt Marj to keep going. And you owe it to yourself, too. You get down on yourself way too easily. Some guy says you're an awful athlete and you go, 'Oh, okay, I guess I am.' *No!* What you do is, you say, 'Oh, yeah? I'll show you you're wrong!' You think Van Sluman is a better athlete than you are? He's just more self-confident, period."

Theo shook his head. "I don't know. . . ."

"*I* know," insisted Paul. "Listen, Gee, don't let what happened today turn you around. You have to *use* it to give you another reason to keep working. If you need something else to think about while you work out, think of Van Sluman pushing that peanut down Main Street. On a hot summer day. While you watch."

Theo laughed. "Yeah, I'd love to see that. Okay, you're right. I'll keep going. I'll be out here in the park tomorrow."

"And the next day . . . ," Paul said.

"And the day after that," Theo went on.

"All *right!*" Paul said, reaching out a clenched fist. "Want some company tomorrow?"

Theo smiled. "Absolutely."

6

I'm really going to push myself today," said Theo. He and Paul were doing their warm-up stretches, before beginning their workout. It was the morning after the disastrous softball game.

"What do you mean, 'push yourself'?" asked Paul. "You've already been pushing yourself, you know. You don't want to push yourself too hard, especially today. It's really hot, in case you didn't notice."

Theo *did* notice. Even though it was still pretty early, the thermometer outside the Gordimers' kitchen window had read close to ninety degrees when Theo and Paul had left for the park. It would certainly become hotter during the next hour or so.

"I think I can put more energy into these workouts," Theo said. "I only had to stop once during the running part of my last session. Well, I think I can make it through without stopping at all, if I just refuse to quit. Anyway, that's what I want to do today."

Paul looked unconvinced. "Yesterday, you said that would be your goal for the end of the week. Now you want to do it today. I think you should think again, maybe take it a little easier. Especially in this heat. You could —"

But Theo wasn't ready to listen. "I've been taking it too easy on myself all my life. That's going to stop. Today. I can do it, I know I can."

"You can get heat exhaustion, too," Paul pointed out. "Dad told me what can happen when you make yourself work too hard in really hot weather. It sounds pretty awful. You get weak and dizzy and you can just collapse. This is the first really hot day since you started running. I think it'd be a good idea to work up to it little by little, like you planned to at first.

"Dad says that if you set your goals so high that you can't make them, you just risk getting hurt. The least that'll happen is that you'll be discouraged. If I were you, I'd go a little easy today. If it was cooler, it might make more sense to push like that."

Theo shook his head. "Uh-uh, today I'm going to

walk ten minutes, run ten minutes, and then walk ten minutes. That's it. See, you don't get it, Paul. You're a good athlete. You always have been. Someone like me, who never was any good at sports, I have to work harder at it if I'm going to get anywhere. That's what I have to do, so that's what I'm *going* to do. All right?"

Paul didn't look like he was convinced, but he saw that Theo was not going to change his mind. "All right," he said. "Let's go."

As they started walking, Paul let Theo set the pace, which was fast — faster than Theo had been walking. Even Paul, who *was* a better natural athlete, thought that this was a high speed to begin a workout on a hot day, but he said nothing, not wanting to get into an argument with his friend.

Suddenly, Paul looked at Theo and said, "Yo, Gee, didn't you bring anything to drink?"

Theo realized that he'd forgotten the bottle of sports drink that he usually brought with him and kept in a little canvas bag on a belt. "That's all right," he said, not wanting to stop the session. "I'll be okay without it."

"It's a bad idea not to drink anything when you

work out on a hot day," said Paul. "Look, we can just start again after you get that bottle."

Theo shook his head. "Next time, I'll remember to bring it with me. This time, I'm going to manage without it. I have to toughen up, right? Well, doing without a drink for a half hour is going to help me toughen up. Those guys aren't going to get on my case anymore. Come on!"

So they walked on. Every so often, Paul cast worried glances at Theo. As the walk continued, Theo realized that he had begun to sweat heavily, more so than he usually did at this early stage of a workout. Also, his face felt hot. Well, of course he felt hot, and he was sweating. It was a hot day. It figured that he'd sweat. Good, he'd lose more weight.

"Gee? Yo, Gee! You want a drink?" Theo turned to find Paul holding out a bottle toward him.

Theo shook his head. "No, I'm okay. I don't need it." He kept walking, staring at the path in front of him. Unlike other days when he and Paul were together, Theo didn't feel at all like talking. He realized that he was beginning to breathe harder than he usually did. Well, that was to be expected. It was getting hotter.

Theo had lost all sense of passing time when he heard Paul's watch beep. Ten minutes had gone by, and it was time to start running.

"Here we go," Theo said, trying not to show that he was beginning to pant, and broke into a run. Paul stood motionless, watching him, and then ran to catch up. Theo felt his friend's eyes on him and knew that Paul was getting more and more concerned.

"Listen, Theo, you better slow down and take a drink," Paul said at last.

Theo didn't say anything but waved off Paul's bottle and kept running. His face now felt like it was on fire, and his mouth was very dry. He had no idea how long they'd been running, or how fast they were going. He just knew that he was going to keep running, that he *had* to keep running until he heard Paul's watch beep again and he could finally slow down.

Except he *had* slowed down . . . hadn't he? It was hard to tell. It was so hot, and his mouth was so dry, and he thought he heard Paul calling his name but it sounded very far away, as if Paul were miles and miles away. . . .

"Gee? *Gee!* Hey man, do you hear me?"

Theo blinked. For a moment he didn't know where he was. Only that he felt really awful — sick, hot, and very, very thirsty.

Then he realized that he was lying facedown on the ground.

"Gee?" Paul said, kneeling next to Theo. "Talk to me, dude!"

"Umph," Theo said obediently. He tried to move but found that it was hard to do.

Finally, with Paul's help, Theo was able to turn over and get into a sitting position. Paul spilled a little of the liquid from his bottle onto a handkerchief and put it on Theo's forehead. It felt wonderful. He put the bottle in Theo's hand.

"Take a drink. Just a sip. Do it!"

Theo nodded and swallowed a little of the sports drink. He'd never tasted anything better in his whole life and wanted to gulp it all down, but Paul pulled the bottle away.

"A little at a time," he said. "Now, take a little more, then just rest for a bit."

After another drink, Theo looked around. They

were in a wooded part of the park, and there was nobody else around. Theo sat there, not saying anything, just breathing slowly and trying to clear his head.

A few minutes later, Theo said, "I'm feeling a little better, I think."

"Good," said Paul. "Think you can stand up if I give you a hand?"

"I guess," Theo replied. Slowly, with Paul's help, Theo managed to get to his feet. He swayed a little but stayed upright.

"Wow," he whispered, blinking. "That was . . . *wow.* What happened?"

Paul said, "You were running, sort of. I mean, your arms and legs were moving, but not, like, together. Then you folded. It was like your legs turned into cooked spaghetti. You went down and stayed down. Man, I was scared!"

"But why?" Theo asked.

"It must have been the heat. Plus, you wouldn't take a drink. Call it heat exhaustion or dehydration or both. And you passed out."

Theo licked his lips. "Could I have a little more to drink?"

Paul handed him the bottle. "Take it easy. Just a little, or you could get sick."

Theo drank slowly. He still felt rubbery, but he was beginning to recover.

"There's a bench over there," Paul said, pointing. The bench was under a tree, fifty yards away. "Think you can get there and sit down?"

Theo stared at the bench. It seemed very far away. "Yeah, I think. Let's go."

After what seemed like an endless walk, they got to the bench. Theo sat down heavily and closed his eyes. Paul sat next to him.

"Thanks," Theo said after a few minutes. "You didn't say, 'I told you so.'"

Paul shrugged. "I figured you didn't need me to tell you. I bet you don't forget to bring liquid along again. And that you won't push too hard — especially on a hot day."

Theo laughed weakly. "You win both bets. I was really dumb."

"I won't argue," Paul agreed. "Listen, when you think you're ready, we'll walk back to where we left our bikes. Then we can call and get a lift from there. I think you're better off not trying to ride home."

Theo frowned. "I was sort of hoping not to tell my parents about this. They'd only get worried and upset."

"You sure about that?" Paul asked. "You didn't do anything that was so terrible. You just made a mistake, and it looks like you'll be all right, so why hide it? Then, if they ever do find out, it'll look even worse. I'd call them for a ride, and I'd tell them what happened and that you learned an important lesson."

Theo sighed. "I guess you're right. Let's go back. I think I can make it."

"We'll take it real easy," Paul said.

Theo grinned. "Excellent idea."

It took a lot more time to walk back than it had to get to the place where Theo had collapsed. Theo didn't think he would faint or fall over again, but he still felt sick and feverish.

As they got back to the bikes, Theo saw a public phone and called his house. Mrs. Gordimer answered, and Theo asked for a lift. He gave his mother a short version of what had happened to him and assured her that he was feeling better.

"Well, if you say you're all right, I'll take the van so you can fit your bikes in."

"Thanks, Mom."

When Mrs. Gordimer drove up, she looked concerned, but she brightened when she saw that her son was on his feet. The boys loaded their bikes into the back of the van.

"Maybe it's not a good idea to be too active when the weather's this hot," Mrs. Gordimer said.

"It's usually okay," Paul replied, "as long as you're careful."

"Which I wasn't," added Theo. "But now I know better." He settled back and closed his eyes.

"You learned a valuable lesson, then," Mrs. Gordimer said.

"I sure did," said Theo softly, not opening his eyes. He wasn't sure what the lesson was. Maybe it was that some people aren't meant to be athletes.

7

The next morning, Theo woke up and felt better — but not completely. He was still a little shaky and his face felt hot. Mr. Baskin had called the previous evening and advised Theo not to work out the next day.

"Take it easy and you can probably go back to your regular routine the day after. And, even though you already know this, I'll say it again: *never* go without drinking, especially on a hot day."

"Never again," Theo said. "I was really, really dumb yesterday."

"Don't let it get to you," said Paul's father. "You're not the first person to ever make a mistake. And you can just pick right up where you left off."

"Right," Theo said. "I will."

But that morning, Theo wasn't sure about what he was going to do. He'd had trouble getting to sleep the night before. He'd kept thinking about collapsing in the park and lying there like a jerk. It was embarrassing, even though nobody had seen it happen except Paul.

What would it be like if the same thing happened during the five K? How would he feel if he fainted, or whatever it was, with a whole bunch of runners around him and a lot of people, maybe even his family, watching from the sidelines? It was a horrible thought.

Theo lay back in bed. He wished that he had never said anything about running to Marj. If he wasn't able to run the race, or to finish it, she would be really disappointed. And if he just suddenly quit running, gave it up, she would probably be even more disappointed.

What should he do?

Feeling very sorry for himself, Theo pulled out a video game and started playing. At least he could do something that would let him stop thinking about yesterday and the way he felt today.

He was still playing the game when Paul knocked on his door and peeked inside. Theo didn't know whether he'd been playing the game for half an hour or three hours. He *did* know that he wasn't happy to see Paul. He really didn't feel like seeing anyone at all.

"How you feeling?" asked Paul, coming in with a big smile on his face, like everything in the world was just fine.

"Oh . . . okay," Theo said, reluctantly putting down his joystick and turning off the game player. "I mean, I feel better than yesterday, but I'm not all better. You know."

"Sure," Paul said. "It's a good idea to take the day off. Tomorrow, I bet you're feeling as good as new."

"Probably," Theo said. There was a long, awkward silence. "Uh, listen, I really don't feel like any company right now, okay? You all right with that?"

Paul, who had just sat down in Theo's desk chair, jumped up again. "Sure, no problem. I really only wanted to make sure you were feeling better. See you later, then."

"Right," said Theo, reaching for the joystick.

Paul got as far as the bedroom door and stopped. "I'm leaving," he said, "but I want to say one thing before I go. I hope you're not going to give up your running just because of what happened yesterday. That'd be a huge mistake."

"I haven't given up," Theo replied, feeling a little trapped. "And, even if I did, I don't know if it's such a big mistake."

"Sure it is," Paul insisted. "Look at the progress you made already. It'll get easier if you just keep it up. Really. The more you do it, the better you'll get and the less it'll feel like a huge, heavy load you're carrying and the more it'll feel like fun."

Theo shrugged. "If you say so."

"I *do* say so. Maybe you haven't noticed this yet, but you've lost some weight. It shows in your face. I bet you have pants that you had trouble fitting into that fit just fine now. Well, anyway . . . see you."

Paul waved and left Theo alone in the bedroom.

Theo thought about what Paul had said. He hadn't considered his weight, but now he was curious. He opened his closet and pulled out a pair of new pants that he hadn't gotten around to wearing because they'd felt tight and uncomfortable around the waist. He tried them on. They fit perfectly. Paul was right.

He suddenly felt better. Wearing the new pants, Theo went downstairs, looking for his father. He found Mr. Gordimer in his basement workshop, sanding down a set of bookshelves that he was building.

“Hey, Dad!” Theo trotted down the basement steps. “Check this out!”

Mr. Gordimer put down the sander and looked at his son.

“Remember these pants? How they were too tight when I tried them on? Well, look at them now!”

Theo’s father smiled. “You’re looking good, son. You’ve lost weight. That’s great!”

Theo looked at himself in a mirror leaning against a wall of the workshop. “Yeah, I have. It’s got to be the workouts.”

“Well, that makes sense,” agreed Mr. Gordimer. “You’re more active, burning more calories. Well done, Theo. Keep it up!”

“Thanks, Dad, I will . . . only . . .”

Mr. Gordimer wiped off his hands. “What’s on your mind, Theo? For a guy who’s looking good, you don’t look all that happy.”

Theo wasn’t sure how to say what was on his mind. “Well, I guess I feel a little scared, basically.”

“About what?” Theo’s father walked away from his workbench. “Let’s sit down someplace and talk this out.”

Father and son climbed the stairs and sat in the

living room. "Now then," said Mr. Gordimer, "what are you scared of?"

"What if I can't do this?" Theo asked. "What if I'm getting in too deep? If I can't finish this race, it's going to be bad news. Especially for Aunt Marj. I mean, I *promised* her that I'd do this."

Mr. Gordimer nodded thoughtfully. "Let me talk about this in two parts. First, the thing to remember is that Marj loves you a lot. When you told her that you were going to take up running to enter this race, she was very happy. She still is. And there is absolutely *nothing* you could do that would disappoint her, not now. Just knowing that you're doing your best is all she wants or needs from you. She doesn't expect you to become a running champion overnight. And neither should you.

"That brings me to the second part. You're worrying too much about not being able to finish the race, or that you'll fall over in the middle of it and embarrass yourself and us. In other words, you're worrying about something that won't happen. For what it's worth, I'm betting that you'll run the race and finish it. You have a habit of selling yourself short, and you should try not to do that."

Theo laughed. "I'm not selling myself short. It's just that I know I'm no athlete. That's just knowing the truth when you see it."

His father held up a hand. "You'd be closer to the mark if you said that *you've never been* an athlete, up to now. Which is very different. That doesn't mean that you can't *become* an athlete. The fact is that you've never tried — until now. Now, for the first time, you are trying, and, so far, you're doing better at it. You still don't know what your limits are.

"What you ought to say is: 'I'm an athlete, but I still don't know how good I am.'"

"Five K," Theo said. "That's a long run."

"But you still have lots of time to get ready for it," Mr. Gordimer pointed out. "Also, you can be very strong-minded, when you want to be. You forget how stubborn you can be when you really want to overcome a challenge. Remember when you learned to ride a bike? I lost count of the number of times you fell and scraped your knees and elbows. But every time, you jumped right back on the bike and gave it another shot. You wouldn't quit. You never said, 'Well, I'm just not a bike rider and I never will be.' And you finally did it. I was really proud of you."

Theo grinned. "Did I fall that much?"

"Over and over and over," said his father, smiling at the memory. "And when you had to pass a swimming test to use the deep end of the pool at camp? It was the same deal. It's not like you started out as a great natural swimmer. You worked at it until you had it. Same thing when you had to dive off a diving board. At first you were scared at the idea of diving headfirst off a board. But you didn't let it stop you. You went ahead and did it.

"I think it'll turn out the same way with running. I believe in you, Theo. This is just another one of those challenges that you'll meet and overcome."

Theo felt much better. "I'll sure try," he said. "Thanks, Dad."

Mr. Gordimer ruffled Theo's hair. "I'm just telling it like it is, son."

Theo went to the phone and called Paul. "Listen, I wanted to let you know — I'll be on the school track tomorrow, running again."

"Excellent!" said his friend.

"And I'll follow your dad's schedule. *And* . . . I'll bring plenty to drink."

8

The next day was comfortably cooler, to Theo's relief. He felt healthy and ready to go to work. It helped Theo to know that he had already lost some weight and that he wouldn't be carrying as much fat around the track anymore. He started with his stretches, feeling eager to see what he could do.

According to Mr. Baskin's schedule, today Theo would walk eight minutes. Then he'd walk and run for twelve minutes — making sure that he ran for at least six minutes without stopping — and finish with a fast ten-minute walk.

Theo had had plenty to drink before leaving home and was carrying a bottle of sports drink with him. Also, he had a new watch, a gift from his parents. It had a digital readout and an alarm that could be programmed to beep at intervals. It would let him know when the first eight minutes was up and then the following twelve minutes. He thought it looked really cool on his wrist. His parents had also promised him a new pair of running shoes to replace his old sneakers, which were getting worn out. He'd get advice from Mr. Baskin on what shoes to buy.

Theo liked the idea of dressing and looking like a runner. It might help him to feel more like a runner, and even to *be* a better runner.

It was late in the afternoon, and Theo saw some other people on the track. Some were older and some were younger, including two girls his own age. Most of them, Theo noticed, were running. He felt a little self-conscious as he began walking around the track. Most of the others were zipping past him, even though he was walking at a pretty fast rate. But nobody seemed to pay much attention to the fact that he was walking while they were running — at least nobody said or did anything to show that they found it odd or silly. An older couple, a man and a woman, were also walking, and at about his speed.

Theo was staying on the inside edge of the track, assuming that it didn't make any difference where he walked. Suddenly a voice just behind him shouted out, *"Track!"*

He turned to look, not understanding what was the matter. A slightly older boy came up behind him and swung out to pass him. As he went by, the other boy glared at Theo.

"Don't you know enough to get out of the way?" he yelled, without stopping or slowing down. Theo's face turned red, but he kept walking. He had done something wrong and didn't even know what it had been.

Behind him, he heard another, quieter voice. "When someone yells 'Track,' it means they're faster than you, and you should move to an outside lane to let them go by. That's a basic rule of track running."

The speaker was a young man, thin but with muscular legs. He came up to Theo and slowed down to a walk. "You just getting started? I don't mean today, I mean, are you new to running and jogging and all this stuff?"

Theo nodded. "Yeah. I want to get into running, and this guy told me to start by doing a combination of walking and running and then run more and walk less. Is that a good idea?"

The young man said, “That’s a great way to begin. You don’t want to try to do too much, too fast. That can get you in trouble.”

Theo smiled. “I already found that out the hard way. Have you been running a long time?”

The young man said, “First, let’s get over to the outside edge of the track, okay? I started when I was about your age — what are you, around thirteen? I was twelve.

“When I first got going, I switched from walking to running, just like you’re doing now. It took me about two months before I could run for thirty minutes without stopping. Now I run six days a week, and I love it. I hope I can keep doing it till I’m ninety. My name is Steve, by the way, Steve LaMotta.”

“Theo Gordimer. Nice to meet you.”

“How come you want to be a runner? If you don’t mind my asking.”

Theo definitely didn’t mind. He explained about wanting to be in better shape, and told Steve about Aunt Marj, her illness, and the five-K race he was hoping to enter.

“Those sound like excellent reasons for wanting to run — not that there’s such a thing as a bad reason.”

"You think I can do it — be ready to run five K in two and a half months?" asked Theo. "Sometimes it sounds crazy to me."

Steve shook his head. "It's not crazy at all. I mean, you don't have any notions of winning the race or setting some kind of record, do you? Only to enter and hopefully finish it?"

"That's it," Theo replied.

"No reason you can't, if you commit to it and work on it," said Steve.

"Do you run races?" Theo asked.

"Yeah," Steve said. "Longer ones . . . ten K, twenty K, marathons."

"Marathons!" Theo said. "That's pretty long, right?"

Steve laughed. "Yeah, pretty long. A marathon is twenty-six-point-two miles — more than forty kilometers."

Theo gulped. "That's amazing. I heard of marathons, but I thought that people who ran them were, like, superheroes. But you look ordinary . . . I mean . . ." He stopped talking, feeling a little foolish.

Steve laughed. "I left my superhero costume at home today. But seriously, most of the good runners I know look pretty ordinary."

The guy who had yelled at Theo earlier came up alongside Theo and Steve. He sneered at them. "If you want to walk, why don't you find a sidewalk? Tracks are for runners!"

"Chill out," said Steve, smiling. "Nobody's stopping you from running."

"Well, this kid was walking on the inside lane before," the guy said.

"He's new, and he made a mistake," replied Steve. "It won't happen again. Why don't you just get over it and leave him alone? Go on and run."

The other guy looked like he wanted to say something more, but finally he just sneered again and took off down the track. Steve watched him go.

"Don't pay any attention to guys like that," he said. "You find a few like him everywhere, in any sport — and not only in sports. Don't ever let them get to you. That guy probably doesn't feel good unless he can make someone else feel bad. You have as much right to be here as he does, and don't forget that. Was that you, beeping just now?"

"Yeah, that was my watch," Theo said. "It's time for me to run."

"Okay, then," said Steve. "Don't push yourself too hard. I'll be seeing you around. Nice meeting you, Theo."

"You, too," Theo said. "And thanks."

Steve speeded up and took off, waving good-bye as he did. Theo took a drink and began to run, encouraged by the fact that this Steve, who was a really good runner, had started in much the same way that he was doing now.

As he ran, Theo actually passed a few others on the track, including the two older walkers. By the time he felt tired enough to slow down to a walk, he checked his watch to find that he'd been running for six and a half minutes and had covered two and a half laps. He walked for a minute and then ran again until his watch beeped and it was time for his last ten-minute walk.

In that ten minutes, Theo walked three quarters of a mile. Afterward, he drank again and did his stretches. Steve caught his eye, running past, and gave Theo a thumbs-up signal. The boy who'd given Theo a hard time was also still on the track but ignored him, which was fine.

Theo felt tired but not wiped out. It had been a good workout. He'd met a good runner who'd given him advice and encouragement. He'd learned a little about good manners on a track. And he'd run a little farther and a little faster than he had before. That made it an excellent day.

That evening, Theo dropped by to see Paul. Mr. Baskin came out to where the boys were sitting in the backyard. "How are you doing, Theo? Have you recovered from what happened the other day?"

Theo nodded. "Yeah, I had a good run on the track today. I ran for more than six minutes, nonstop, and I felt really good. Also, I met this really nice guy who's a good runner, and he helped me."

"How did he help, Gee?" asked Paul.

"He told me that you shouldn't run on the inside lane of a track unless you're really fast, and he told me he got started doing the same things your dad told me to do. Also, when this kid got on my case because I was walking, Steve told him to get lost."

Paul said, "Steve was the really good runner?"

"Yeah, he was really nice," Theo answered. "And he runs long distances, too."

Mr. Baskin asked, "Did you get his last name?"

"Uhh . . ." Theo thought for a moment. "LaMotta. That was it. Steve LaMotta."

Mr. Baskin's eyes widened. "You met *Steve LaMotta* on the school track?"

"Who is he, Dad?" Paul asked.

"Steve LaMotta is one of the top American distance runners! He runs in major meets, ten thousand meters, twenty thousand meters, and marathons. Wait a minute, I have something to show you."

Mr. Baskin hurried into the house. Paul and Theo exchanged a look.

"Guess this Steve is someone special," Theo said.

Paul smiled. "Special enough so Dad's heard of him and got real excited. I never saw him like that."

"Here we are," said Paul's father, coming outside carrying a magazine. He opened it up and leafed through it. "This is a running magazine I get every month. . . . Wait a sec. . . . Here we go." He handed the open magazine to Theo. "Is this the man you met today?"

Theo stared. The magazine was opened to a full-page ad for a brand of running shoe. Most of the page was taken up by a big color photograph of a runner crossing the finish line on a track. In the background was a huge grandstand full of people. The runner in the picture was breaking a tape stretched across the track, which meant that he had won the race. The runner in the picture was Steve LaMotta! Steve LaMotta was a star! He endorsed a brand of shoe! And he had started out just like Theo!

Theo's next big day was during his third week of running, when he ran three quarters of a mile — three whole laps around the track! — without a stop. It was a hot day, too, about the same kind of day on which he'd collapsed not long before. But he knew enough now to be sure to drink often, and didn't try to push too hard. He was walking faster and expected to be able to run a full mile very soon.

One day soon after, Paul mentioned that he was going to the park the next day to play some ball. "I don't know whether you want to go, after what happened last time. . . ."

"Sure!" Theo said. Paul was surprised by Theo's enthusiasm. Actually, Theo was a little surprised himself. But he wanted to go. He was feeling different about himself, less worried about making mistakes.

"Great!" Paul said. "Come by here tomorrow at two o'clock and we'll ride over."

Theo shook his head. "I'm going to run in the park first. I'll meet you there."

"Okay," Paul agreed. "If you want, I can stop by your place and bring your glove."

"That'd be cool," said Theo. "See you at two o'clock at the field."

The next day, Theo rode to the park, did his stretches, and walked the first eight minutes, feeling wonderful. It was a warm, pleasant day, and Theo was able to enjoy himself as he walked. He looked at the scenery, listened to the birds, and breathed deeply and easily. He was actually looking forward to playing softball. He smiled to himself. A month ago, if someone had told him, "You're going to look forward to playing ball," Theo would have laughed.

His watch beeped, and Theo took a swallow from the bottle at his side. He broke into a run. Maybe he could make it for ten minutes without a break today. But at the nine-minute mark, Theo felt like he was beginning to breathe too hard and decided not to try for ten whole minutes. Thirty seconds later, he slowed to a walk. Maybe, if he hadn't been planning to play ball later, he might have gone for the ten minutes. But he wanted to have plenty of energy left for the game. If he messed up today, it wouldn't be because he was wiped out.

Theo walked for ten minutes, finishing up near the field where the ballgame was going to happen, which was where he'd left his bike. He did his stretches; he no longer had to bring Mr. Baskin's diagrams, because he knew all the stretches by heart. He spotted Paul's bike nearby and headed that way.

Paul and some others were standing in a big circle and tossing a softball around. Paul looked up and saw Theo coming and smiled. So did Van Sluman. Van's smile was different from Paul's. Van looked more like a cat that had just spotted a tasty bird nearby.

"Hey, Gee, how's it going?" Paul asked, sticking out a hand for a low five.

"How's the Great Runner doing?" Van asked, looking around to his friends and inviting them to get in on the fun. "Broken four minutes for a mile yet? Run any marathons?"

Theo smiled back, not looking upset at all. "Not yet."

One of the others looked Theo up and down. "Hey, Gordimer, you losing weight?"

"Yeah, you look thinner," said another.

Theo was pleased. He shrugged. "I lost a few pounds. That's what happens when you start burning up more calories."

"Oh, right, you're burning up calories, huh?" Van said. "All those workouts, huh?"

Theo nodded. "That, and I'm not eating as much junk food lately, either."

Paul grinned at Van. "You know what junk food is, right, Van? Stuff like peanuts. By the way, have you started practicing pushing that peanut with your nose yet? It's a long way from one end of Main Street to the other. Better pick up some knee pads, too."

A few of the guys snickered, and Van's smirk lost some of its power.

"Are you really running, Gordimer?" asked the boy who had first noticed Theo's weight loss.

"Yeah, most days. It's pretty cool, I really like it."

"How far do you run?" the boy asked.

Theo shrugged. "In the park, it's hard to know, exactly. Further than I used to, and not as far as I'll be able to next month."

"We going to just stand around, or are we going to play ball?" snapped Van.

"I vote we play ball," Theo said. They chose up sides, and Theo was the last one to be picked. He wasn't surprised or even disappointed. Even though he was working at getting into better shape, nobody had any reason to figure that he was any better as a ballplayer.

For the first inning, Theo did nothing to change anyone's opinion of him — because he didn't get a chance to bat and because no balls were hit in his direction.

But in the second inning, an opposing hitter did hit a ball to right, hard, with a runner at first and only one out. It seemed a sure extra-base hit; with Theo huffing and puffing after it, it might have been a home run. But Theo turned his back to the infield and ran, looking back over his shoulder, reached out his glove . . . and *caught* it. The base runner, like everyone else on both teams, had been sure that the hit would be at least a double. He was almost to third base when he looked around and saw what had happened. Theo threw to first to complete a double play before the runner could get halfway back.

As he trotted in from the outfield, Theo wore a big smile. He couldn't remember the last time he'd made a good play in one of these games. Maybe he never had.

Later on, Theo hit a ball into left center for a base hit. When the batter after him hit a line drive that got between two outfielders, Theo raced around to score. It was another first for him. He noticed that other kids were looking at him with surprise. Van Sluman was suddenly very quiet.

As the game went on, Theo didn't suddenly turn into a star. But he played solidly, made no horrible mistakes, and made a few more catches. He thought that maybe the next time they chose up teams, somebody else might be the last one to be picked.

After the game, Theo and Paul rode their bikes home. As they rode, Paul said, "Pretty good game today."

"Yeah, it was, I guess," Theo answered.

"You *guess?*" Paul laughed. "Cut it out."

Theo joined in the laughter. "Okay, I *don't* guess. I played better."

"A lot better," agreed Paul. "That running catch you made saved at least one run. And coming all the way around from first to score! I felt like asking, 'Who *is* that guy, and what has he done with Gee?' "

"I'm definitely faster," Theo admitted.

"That's true," said Paul, "but it's something else, too. A month ago, you wouldn't even have tried to catch that ball. It isn't only a matter of running faster. You were . . . more sure of yourself today. You can see that, can't you?"

Theo said, "You're right. It's true. Part of it is that I feel stronger and better since I started running. And part is something Steve LaMotta said when I met him.

"There was this guy running on the track who gave me a hard time because I did something stupid. I didn't know what I was doing, so I was on the inside of the track, which is supposed to be for the faster runners. And I wasn't even running at the time. Later on, Steve said, 'Guys like that don't feel good unless they can make someone else feel bad.'

"When Van started ragging me today, I remembered that. Van's the same kind of guy. I knew that if I let it show that it bothered me, Van would win. So I didn't. And you know what? It didn't bother me."

"Because you know yourself better than Van knows you," Paul said. "You really have changed, Gee."

Theo grinned. "Maybe. But I haven't changed so much that I didn't enjoy seeing Van look nervous about losing our bet."

After getting home and cleaning up, Theo phoned Marj and asked if she wanted any company. His aunt didn't sound wonderful but said she'd be happy to see him for a little while.

Marj was sitting up, which was good to see, but she seemed in very low spirits. She said to Theo, "You're looking good, young man. You're thinner and your skin has some color. You used to look like something that lived in tunnels underground and never got out in the sun."

"Well, I've gotten out of my tunnel," Theo agreed. "I'm running and doing much better. I played softball today and didn't do anything terrible. How are you feeling?"

Marj closed her eyes. "Not all that great. I won't

lie to you, Theo. I'm tired of feeling tired. It gets old, you know what I mean?"

"Sure, I understand," Theo said. "But what I learned from what I've been doing is that it's important to keep a good attitude. Really. And don't give up. I played better ball today because I wasn't thinking of myself like a loser. So you should try to keep thinking about how great it will be when you're all better. It really helps. It sure helped me. And you know what? You *do* look better. You even sound better. I mean, you're sitting up and you have a sense of humor again. You may think I'm crazy, but I can tell you're doing all right."

"That's what you think?" Marj asked. "You're not just being nice to an old lady?"

"I mean it," Theo insisted. "You look stronger to me, even if you are tired. I bet you'll be feeling much better real soon — if you don't give up and quit."

Marj said, "Hey! Who's coaching who around here?"

"I'm just saying what I think," Theo said. "And I think you're doing pretty well. And that you can help yourself even more."

Marj's expression seemed more cheerful than when Theo had arrived. "Listen, smart guy, do me a favor."

"Sure," Theo said. "Anything."

"Stop by here more often, will you? You cheer me up."

"You got it," Theo said.

"And keep giving me those kind words. They make a difference. It's hard to believe, but I actually feel better now."

"Good," Theo said happily. "See you soon, then. Maybe we'll be able to take a walk one of these days."

"I wouldn't be surprised," said Marj.

During his fourth week of workouts, Theo ran a full mile on the track without a stop. He ran it in about ten and a half minutes. After his final stretches, he did something else he'd never done: he touched his toes without bending his knees. A five-K run was looking more and more possible.

Theo had gotten new running shoes, the first pair of actual running shoes he'd ever owned. They made a difference. They were light, and his feet and ankles felt better when he used them. His parents celebrated his achievement by taking him out to dinner.

Theo was now in his fifth week of running and had set himself a goal. He wanted to run a mile and a half, nonstop. This week, he would be running for up to fifteen minutes, which made the mile and a half something he might really do.

After a few days in the park, Theo went to the track to run. A mile and a half meant six full laps, and today he was going to go for it. He stretched and warmed up with a five-minute walk. The day was cloudy and cool, so Theo wasn't worried about the heat tiring him out. He finished his prerun drink, took a deep breath, and began to run.

He finished two laps with no strain at all, but midway through the third, Theo began feeling as if he was pushing himself. Was it possible that he'd set his goal too high, too soon? He wasn't going to give up easily.

As he ran, Theo heard a familiar voice behind him. "Hey, Theo! Looking good!"

It was Steve LaMotta, who came up and slowed down to Theo's pace. "You're doing much better than when I saw you last. Congratulations!"

"Thanks," Theo said. "I think I might be shooting for too much today, though."

"Can I make a suggestion?" Steve asked.

"Sure!" Theo answered.

"You need to relax a little," Steve said. "Especially

your arms and hands. Do you know that your fists are clenched and your arms are tense like you're getting ready for a wrist-wrestling match? That just tires you out, and it doesn't help your running at all."

Startled, Theo realized that he *was* doing exactly what Steve said. And just focusing on it made him a little more tired.

"Loosen up those arms. Shake 'em out. Keep them relaxed and loose. Try to imagine that you're holding a tennis ball in each hand so you don't clench your fists. You'll find that running is much less strain," Steve said. "And while we're at it, I think you're doing something we call 'overstriding.' Your stride — the length of your steps — is too long, and that adds to the strain, too. Try to shorten your stride by an inch or two and your legs may feel more comfortable."

Theo thought for a moment and tried to cut down the length of his steps by a little.

"Experiment a bit," Steve advised. "Find a stride that feels right. You'll know when you have it."

As he ran, Theo tried to find a stride that would make a difference. He'd run a hundred or so yards and change it a bit. Finally, after four or five changes, he looked over at Steve. "I think I got it! This does feel more natural."

"Great!" Steve said. "One last thing — if I'm not making you crazy with all this."

"No, what is it?" Theo asked, feeling more comfortable with his relaxed arms and slightly shorter stride.

"I think your neck and shoulders are too tight, too," Steve said. "When you run any distance, the idea is not to waste energy on muscles that you don't need. Also, if you tense up in the wrong places, you get really sore. You need to do some posture work to take some of the pressure off your neck. I can show you a few things. But for now, it looks like you're not having as much trouble as you were."

"You're right — I'm not." Theo was pleased, and even more so to realize that, as he and Steve had been together, they'd gone two more laps. He was within one lap of his mile and a half — and he actually felt less worn out than after a half mile!

Steve took off, telling Theo he'd see him around, and Theo finished the final lap of the mile and a half. He made a mental note of something else he'd learned today: you tended to not feel so tired if you didn't think about being tired.

When he got home, Mrs. Gordimer said, "Let's go shopping. All your old pants are falling off you now, and when you wear a belt to keep them up, they look awful."

Theo had always hated shopping for clothes. Today, however, he was happy to go. New pants with a smaller waistline sounded like a great idea.

"I'll get cleaned up, and I'll be ready in a few minutes."

And he *raced* up the stairs.

11

Two weeks after Theo's first mile-and-a-half run, he and Paul started running together regularly. Theo had now been running almost two months. From the days when he was walking ten minutes, doing ten minutes of run-and-walk, and walking ten minutes more, he had reached the point where he was now mostly running. His walking totaled only a few minutes of warmup to start with and a few minutes at the end of his run, to cool down.

Also, Theo had begun to run two and a half miles in a session, which was what Paul was doing. They were together today, running in the park along a path that was popular with local runners.

"Have you gotten to where you actually enjoy running?" Paul asked. "Or is it still a grind, something you feel you have to do?"

"No, I really enjoy it," Theo said. "I don't know when it happened exactly, but I've gotten so that I look forward to it. Even when I push myself, it's still fun."

"I won't say, 'I told you so,'" said Paul, "but . . ."

Theo smiled. "You don't have to say it. I already know. Maybe I might have gotten started on something like this anyway, but it would have taken a long time. You and your dad made it happen for me."

Paul laughed. "No, *you* made it happen for you. But I know we helped get you going, and I feel good about that. So does Dad. Have you tried running five K yet?"

"Not yet, but soon," said Theo. "For sure I'll do it in a couple of weeks. That would leave me about two weeks more to get ready for the race. I suppose I'd run the full distance a few more times before the big day."

"I was thinking," Paul said, as the two boys ran on, "maybe I want to be in that race, too. I mean, it's for a good cause, and it'd be fun to do it together. What do you think?"

Theo was surprised and pleased. "I think that's a fantastic idea! And I know Aunt Marj would be really happy to hear about it. I'll tell her next time I talk to her."

"How's she doing?" asked Paul.

Theo shrugged. "A little better. I think she's a little stronger lately. But she gets real depressed about not being able to do more, and that kind of sets her back. I try to see her at least every few days. She likes company, but she still gets tired pretty fast."

The boys heard someone calling from behind them. "Hey, Theo! Is that you?"

Theo looked back to see Steve LaMotta quickly catching up to them. He came even with them and slowed to their pace. "I thought I saw you running. You're doing better every time I see you." Steve caught Paul's eye and nodded. "Hi," he said.

"Steve, this is my friend, Paul Baskin. He's the guy who got me started in running."

"Good to meet you, Paul," said Steve.

"Good to meet *you!*" replied Paul. "Wait'll I tell my dad about this! He's into running, big-time. He's read all about you."

"Maybe I can meet him sometime," Steve said. "Oh, by the way, that race you're going to enter — is that the one for cancer research next month?"

“That’s the one,” said Theo.

Steve nodded. “Yeah, I thought so. It turns out I’m going to be the official starter.”

“Great!” Theo said. “I was wondering, how does it work? Where do they — I mean *we* — run, anyway?”

“It’s a road course,” said Steve. “The runners will start in the park here. Most of the course will be on local streets. Then you’ll come back into the park for the last few hundred meters and finish here. I can get you a map of the course, if you like. Then you could actually run it and get to know it a little before the race.”

“That sounds like a good idea,” Paul said.

“Tell you what,” said Steve. “Let’s plan to meet the day you sign up to enter the race. I’ll give you the map then.”

“When can we sign up?” asked Theo.

“Starting next week, either at the high school or in the park administration building.” Steve reached into the little pack he wore on a belt along with his drinking bottle and pulled out a card. “You can reach me at this phone number, and we’ll work out a day and time for you to sign up and for me to meet you.”

Theo took the card and tucked it into the pocket of the T-shirt he was wearing. "Great! Thanks a lot!"

"Yeah, thanks," Paul said.

Steve smiled. "No problem. I like to see young guys like you getting into running like this. When I can do anything for you, I will. But now I'd better take off. See you later!"

He picked up his pace without the slightest show of effort and sped away. Theo and Paul, still running, watched him go.

"Amazing!" Paul said. "He's like a total machine! No strain, no pain. What a smooth stride the guy has!"

Theo nodded. "Well, he runs marathons and twenty-thousand-meter races. By the way, how come sometimes they say, 'ten thousand meters' or 'twenty thousand meters,' and sometimes they say, 'ten K' or 'twenty K'? Don't they mean the same thing?"

Paul replied, "I asked my dad about that. He says that when you run long-distance races on a track, they measure them in meters, like five thousand meters or ten thousand meters. But for road races, like the one we're doing, they talk about them in kilometers — five K or ten K."

"Huh. Somehow, five thousand meters seems

longer than five K." Theo looked at his watch. "We've been running for twenty minutes. Amazing! I didn't realize we'd been going so long."

Paul looked around. "We're not too far from where we left our bikes. Let's head that way and walk the last few minutes."

The boys had parked their bikes near the ball field. When they got to the bikes, they noticed some boys they knew at the field.

"Looks like they're going to play," Paul said. "Want to go over, or are you wiped out?"

"I'm not wiped out," Theo said, "but we don't have gloves or anything."

"We can borrow someone else's gloves when they're at bat and we're in the field," answered Paul. "I've done that before. Let's go!"

As Theo and Paul came over, the other guys greeted them.

"You got room for two more?" Theo asked.

"Sure," said one of the others.

Theo saw Van Sluman standing off to one side, looking uncomfortable. Theo nodded to him but didn't say anything. Van slowly approached. "Can I talk to you for a second?" he asked Theo.

"Sure."

Van glanced at the other boys out of the corner of his eye. "Uh, how's the running going?" He didn't sound sarcastic at all.

"Pretty good," Theo said. "Better."

Van didn't seem to know what to say. Finally, he took a deep breath. "Listen, about what I said before . . . I was only . . . I didn't mean . . . well, I was wrong. To say what I did. I'm sorry. It was really dumb."

Theo, too, felt a little awkward and wasn't sure how to respond. "Okay," he said at last. "It *was* dumb. But let's just forget about it. I mean, I'm willing to drop it."

Van let out a deep sigh of relief. "You are? That's really great! Thanks! And, um, about that stupid bet . . ."

Theo couldn't help grinning. "Oh yeah, the thing about pushing a peanut with your nose down Main Street. Forget that, too."

"Right," said Van, nodding and smiling. "Okay, hey, thanks, really. I was really a jerk, and I want you to know that I feel bad about it."

Theo felt uncomfortable about the way Van was acting. He wanted to drop the subject.

"Well, like I said, I'd rather just forget the whole thing, all right?"

"Sure," said Van. "Absolutely."

"Come on, you guys!" called one of the other boys. "Let's play!"

As the group chose up sides, Paul whispered to Theo, "What did Van want?"

Theo whispered back, "He says he's sorry he was such a jerk before, and does he really have to push that peanut with his nose. I told him to forget the whole thing."

Paul smirked. "Why? It would've been fun to see that."

Theo said, "I don't want to be a jerk just because he was one."

"I guess you're right," admitted Paul.

When teams were chosen, Theo wasn't among the last to be picked. The team captain asked him to play first base. Van, who was on the opposing team, ran over to offer Theo the use of his glove.

Paul caught Theo's eye and winked.

At first base, Theo was much more involved in the action and caught just about everything thrown his way. He made one really nice play on a ground ball hit to his right, making a diving catch and tossing the ball to the pitcher covering the base.

In his first at bat, Theo hit the ball sharply up the middle. The center fielder trotted over to pick it up, and Theo surprised everyone by stretching the hit into a double when the fielder made a casual throw in.

Later in the game, Theo dropped a throw from shortstop. He was angry with himself and said to the shortstop, "Sorry, I should've had that."

The shortstop said, "It was a tough throw. We'll get 'em out."

The next batter popped the ball up behind first, and Theo backpedaled to make the catch. He realized that he wasn't a star, on offense or defense. But he was also far from a total disaster. And he was having a great time.

Late in the game, one of Theo's teammates ran on a fly ball with only one out. When the ball was caught, the runner had gone too far and was doubled up at first base.

“Real smart, Jeff,” someone yelled.

“Did you leave your brain at home this morning?” shouted another teammate.

Jeff looked at his feet as a few other comments were thrown his way. Theo said nothing. When his team ran back out onto the field, Theo came up to Jeff. “Don’t worry, it’s no big deal,” he said quietly. Jeff smiled at him.

After the game, Theo and Paul were riding home. “I noticed you with Jeff after he messed up,” Paul said. “What did you tell him?”

“Just not to worry about it.”

Paul nodded. “Huh. And you didn’t want to rub it in with Van, either.”

Theo said, “Well, I remember what it felt like when people said stuff like that to me. I almost got into it like that today. But then I couldn’t do it. I wouldn’t have felt right. You know?”

“Yeah,” said Paul. “I know. Now that you’ve explained it to me.”

A few days later, Theo called Steve LaMotta to set a date and time when he and Paul would sign up for the race and meet Steve to get the route map. They set it for one day the following week.

"Has your friend ever raced before?" asked Steve. "I know *you* haven't."

"Uh-uh," Theo said. "It'll be the first time for both of us."

"Then I'll give you a few tips about things you may want to do to get ready for this one," said Steve.

"We'd like that," said Theo. "Thanks."

Then he called Marj.

"Hey, there," she said. She sounded better than when he'd last spoken to her. "Got a little time to spend with me? I could use some company."

"Sure," Theo agreed. He biked over and found Marj sitting on her front porch.

She waved to him as he came up the steps. "Hi, skinny. You're looking good."

Theo smiled and studied his aunt. "You're looking good, too." She really was. Her face had more color, and her smile seemed to be more genuine.

"Let's take a walk," she said. "I've been trying to get a little exercise every day lately."

"Great," Theo said. Marj grabbed a cane from the floor, and Theo helped her down the front steps. They set off down the sidewalk at a slow pace.

"It looks like your workouts are going well," Marj said.

"They are," Theo agreed. He told her about his running, his general improvement in sports, and also about Steve LaMotta. "He's a great guy. Paul and I are going to meet him when we sign up for the race. Paul's racing, too, did I tell you?"

"I'm glad to hear that," Marj replied. "And I want to thank you for your pep talk a while back. It made a difference."

"Yeah?" Theo was pleased and surprised.

Marj said, "Definitely. Keeping a positive attitude turns out to be important for me. I think it's important for anyone in my situation not to get down.

When I get better — did you notice I said *when*, and not *if?* — I'm going to do volunteer work with women going through what I went through. Maybe I can help them learn what I've learned about eating right, taking care of themselves — and especially about keeping their spirits up."

"That sounds like a great plan," said Theo.

"Speaking of plans, do you have any plans about getting into other sports?" Marj asked. "I hear you say that you're playing ball more and enjoying it. Have you thought about going out for any organized sports? Football, baseball? I think that organized sports are great for a lot of kids. Not just because you can stay in good shape, but you can also learn about what it is to be part of a team."

"I know you're right, but the thing I really like right now is running," Theo said. "I could see going out for track or cross-country, maybe. I don't know about other sports. I'm not sure I want to do any of that. And I don't know whether I'll be good enough to make any teams. All I know now is I'm going to keep running."

"I know you, young man," Marj said. "If you set your mind to something, you'll do it. And that includes making a team."

"Well, we'll see," Theo said. "Like I said, I haven't thought about it much. But maybe. Paul wants to play football, but I haven't thought about it."

Marj patted Theo's arm. "Well, there's no need to rush into anything. It's just something to think about. I'd like to head back now," said Marj. "I've enjoyed this, but I have to take it a little at a time."

They went back to Marj's place. Theo helped Marj up the steps.

"Thank you," she said, sitting back down in her chair with a sigh. "I'm doing what you've been doing: adding a little more to my exercise each day."

"That's the way to go," Theo said. "You'll be doing all the stuff you used to do soon, I'll bet."

Marj smiled. "Could be you're right. I believe I'll be a lot stronger than I am now, anyway. How much longer is it until that race?"

"Almost three weeks," Theo said.

"Right now, my plan is to be able to go to watch that race with your mom and dad. I want to be there and root for you and your friend. I think I can do it."

"If you want to, I bet you will," Theo said. "And it'll be fantastic if you do."

Marj smiled at Theo. "I'll be there. You wait and see."

13

On the day arranged for the meeting, Theo and Paul went to the park administration building to sign up for the race. They filled out forms and paid entry fees — donated by their parents — that would go to fund cancer research. They were given papers with the rules for the race and also got official race T-shirts. These were gold with the name of the race in bright red on the back and front.

"You can come in and get your race numbers on the day of the race or the day before," said the woman at the entry table. "You have to wear those numbers on your shirts so we know that you've paid the fee and are officially entered."

Steve was waiting just outside the building when Theo and Paul came out. "I like those shirts," he said when they showed him their new tees. "Here's the map of the route. There aren't many steep hills around here, so it's pretty flat. There's one fairly long rise, but the grade isn't bad. Look it over later."

"Thanks a lot," said Theo. "Uh, you said something about training tips. . . ."

Steve grinned. "Right, I did. I even wrote them out for you. Here." He handed each of them a sheet of paper with printed notes on it. "Let me explain these.

"First, you should do a couple of runs of more than five K, the distance of the race, a couple of times before the race itself — but not during the few days *just* before. I think you might run — let's see . . . thirteen or fourteen laps around the track on those. That works out to a little more than five K, either three and a quarter or three and a half miles. That'll help your stamina on race day.

"Once a week, do what we call speed workouts on the track. In a speed workout, you run a lap around the track as fast as you can, then jog or walk for a one-minute rest interval, then another fast quarter, another one-minute rest, and so on. Do eight or more laps that way, if you can. And remember — when you're walking or jogging, go to the outside edge of the track."

"What do speed workouts do?" asked Theo.

"They help your muscles build up their capacity to take in oxygen. That means you can use your energy more efficiently. It's called 'building your VO_2 max.' You may want to make speed drills part of your regular running routine, not just when you're getting ready for a race. You can gradually add more fast laps, or try doing fast half miles instead of quarters, once you've done it for a while.

"Another thing. The day after a speed workout, do a slower run for variety and to give yourself a little rest.

"Now, let's see . . . you'll be doing one speed workout a week, one long run on the track a week, one easy workout a week. Another thing to try on a long run in the park is to *vary* your speed. Run fairly slow for a few minutes, then speed up, then slow down again, and so on. There may be times in a race when you want to lay back and conserve your energy. Then there may be times when you want to really put the hammer down, put on speed. You may want to pass someone at the end of a race, or psych another runner in the middle of a race and get him or her to try to keep up with you and risk burning himself or herself out. Any questions?"

Theo and Paul looked at each other. They both shook their heads.

"Okay, then," Steve said. "Good luck, and I'll see you on race day. If you want to ask me anything before then, you can leave messages for me at that number I gave Theo."

"Thanks a lot," said Paul.

"Forget it," Steve said. "Have fun."

The next day, Theo and Paul went to the track to try a speed workout, following Steve's suggestions. They found that Paul could run faster quarters than Theo could, by several seconds. But Paul could only manage eight really fast laps. Theo was able to run another lap at his slightly slower pace. He had a little more stamina than Paul, though Paul had more speed.

Two days later, taking the map of the course, Theo and Paul ran and finished the course, not fast, but without stopping. They stayed together, and finished the five kilometers in a little more than twenty-nine minutes, by Theo's watch.

Afterward, breathing heavily, Theo said, "That's as fast as I can do it, for now anyway."

Paul thought for a moment. "I think I could have maybe done it in fifteen or twenty seconds less. I still had a little gas in the tank at the end there."

"But I bet I can cut my time down by race day," Theo added.

"Me, too," said Paul. "A little, for sure."

Both boys were wearing the official race T-shirts. "Hey, let's show the shirts to Aunt Marj," Theo suggested.

They stopped by Marj's place going home. Marj, who had just come back from her daily walk, said that the shirts were "very cool."

The following week, they kept the same schedule. They each added a lap to their speed workouts and ran the laps a bit faster. They also added another lap to their long workouts, doing a full three and a half miles. They took it fairly slow but put on a few bursts of higher speed. Theo ran the last two hundred yards as fast as he could and surprised Paul, who was coasting, by passing him just at the end.

"Hey!" Paul yelled. "Where'd you come from?"

"That was my big finish," Theo said, as they began their cooldown walk.

Theo went to a couple of ball games in the park

during the last weeks before the race. The other players, who by now were all aware of Theo's running, kept asking how it was going. Theo didn't talk about it with them too much. He'd say that he was doing better and not go into detail. He had become a pretty good ballplayer, neither among the best nor the worst of the group who came there.

Four days before the race, Paul and Theo ran sixteen laps around the track — four full miles. It was the farthest either of them had run and the longest time, too: about thirty-three minutes.

Steve had advised them on his information sheet to take it easy the last few days before the race, so they did no more really heavy workouts after the four-miler. Theo felt stronger and in better shape than ever. There was no longer any doubt in his mind about finishing the race.

One night before race day, the Gordimers and Baskins got together for a barbecue cookout in the Gordimer's backyard.

"Don't pig out, now," warned Mr. Baskin. "It's okay to have a big dinner, but don't eat so much that you have trouble getting to sleep. You need your rest."

"Theo doesn't eat like he used to," said Mrs.

Gordimer. "I remember when he'd come to one of these barbecues and eat everything that wasn't nailed down. But lately, he stops when he feels full."

"Actually, I'm full now," Theo said.

"No room for apple pie?" asked Mrs. Baskin.

"Well, I guess I can handle a piece," Theo admitted.

"My mom's pie?" said Paul. "You better believe it!"

Mr. Gordimer shook his head, as if he was still surprised at the change in his son. "We just put a load of his old clothes in a box and put it into a clothes drop at the supermarket. They were just enormous on him."

"Is Marj going to be there tomorrow?" asked Mr. Baskin.

Mrs. Gordimer replied, "She hopes she can make it. But we won't know for sure until the morning."

"I'll bet she's there," Theo said.

"You know how much she wants to be there," said Theo's mother. "Just don't be too disappointed if she doesn't feel up to it. You know that she'll be there in spirit."

Theo nodded. "I know. But I still bet she'll be there."

At seven forty-five the next morning, Theo walked outside to wait for the Baskins, who would take him to the park for the race. Theo's parents would come later — with Marj, Theo hoped.

He'd had breakfast and had on his running clothes and shoes. It was already warm, and would be hot later on. Theo took a drink while he waited, but he wasn't bringing the bottle he usually carried. Mr. Baskin had said that Theo and Paul wouldn't need to bring anything to drink during the race. There would be stations all along the route where volunteers would have cups of water and sports drinks available for runners to take as they ran past.

The Baskins showed up a minute later, and Theo climbed in the backseat.

"Going to be hot," said Paul.

"Right," Mr. Baskin said. "Be sure to drink enough. Use those refreshment stations."

The starting area in the park was busy, even though start time was almost an hour away. Paul and Theo got their numbers and fastened them to their shirts. Theo was 205 and Paul was 206.

"How many people are running?" Paul asked the man with the numbers.

"There are about three hundred fifty signed up," the man. "Plus we'll get some bandits."

Theo and Paul stared at each other. "Bandits?" Theo said.

The man laughed. "That's what we call people who run without signing up or paying the entry fee. They're a nuisance, but you always get some of them. If you see runners who don't have numbers, they're bandits."

As Theo and Paul looked for someplace to stretch, Theo saw runners of all ages getting ready. A few looked about his age. Some looked like they might be in their seventies. There were some in streamlined wheelchairs, with amazingly muscular arms and chests.

Steve LaMotta came by and spotted Theo and

Paul as they were finishing their stretches. "Listen, guys, it's pretty hot. Take it easy at first, don't burn yourselves out early. And drink enough fluid!"

He hurried off. Paul turned to Theo. "You think we should drink anything during the race?"

Theo laughed. "Hey, that sounds like a good idea." He swallowed. "I'm nervous."

Paul was jogging in place. "Me, too."

Theo glanced over to a grandstand that had been set up near the finish line. There were some people sitting there already, but no sign of his parents or Marj, yet.

Theo and Paul talked about nothing in particular for a while. A clock that had been set up near the grandstand said eight forty-five when Steve La-Motta and some other official-looking people got up on a little platform to one side of the grandstand. A man wearing a race T-shirt spoke into a cordless microphone.

"Can I have everyone's attention? We'd like the runners to get into place. We'd like the fastest runners, the ones with numbers under fifty, to go to the front of the field. That way we can avoid traffic jams when we start. Please don't crowd together, everyone.

Runners will be starting at nine o'clock. Wheelchair entrants will start at nine twenty. But first, we have a few people who have things to say."

Other people on the platform spoke, thanking everyone for their contributions to cancer research, thanking the runners for taking part, and thanking the volunteers who had set up the grandstand and platform and were out on the course already, setting up and working the refreshment stations. Finally, the first man introduced Steve LaMotta, who took the mike in one hand and held a starter's pistol in the other.

"Are your folks here?" whispered Paul.

Theo, who had been checking the grandstand often, shook his head. "Not yet."

On the platform, Steve LaMotta said, "I'm pleased to be involved in a race for a worthwhile cause. I hope everyone enjoys themselves today and remembers that running is supposed to be fun. If anyone wants to buy shirts or other race souvenirs, the money will all go to cancer research. And finally — and forgive me if you've heard this already today, but it's important — you runners have to watch out for dehydration on a day like this. Drink lots of fluids. That's all I have to say. Good luck to all. Runners, get set."

He held up the starter's pistol, paused a moment, and fired.

Paul and Theo were toward the back of the crowd of hundreds of runners. It was several seconds after the starting shot before they were able to begin to run. To their left, a boy and a girl who seemed roughly their age took off as if they were in a hundred-meter dash. Without thinking, Theo sped after them.

Paul yelled, "*Hey!* Slow down! Remember what Steve said!"

Feeling a little silly, Theo slowed his pace. "You're right," he admitted.

He and Paul ran together at an easy pace as the field began to stretch out. Some runners took off fast and seemed to whiz by the two boys, while others settled into a jog. Theo and Paul passed several slower ones, but it seemed to Theo like there were more runners ahead of them than behind them. He reminded himself that he had no expectations of winning the race, and that, anyway, some of the ones who were sprinting now might well slow down or even be forced to stop later.

When they found themselves in a shady area, the boys picked up their speed a little. A moment later, they were out of the park and running down a street that had been blocked off for the race. They were in bright, hot sun and slowed down again. Next to Theo was a man who had to be over sixty, but who looked amazingly fit. The man glanced over at Theo and smiled. Theo smiled back, after which the man waved and sped away.

Theo saw a big table a little way ahead, covered with paper cups full of water and sports drinks. Some runners were picking up cups from the table, while others took them from volunteers who were holding them out. Theo and Paul each grabbed a cup from a volunteer and drank the water thirstily. They tossed the cups aside, to be picked up by volunteers.

A moment later, Theo and Paul came to a sign that said 1K. They'd run the first kilometer and had four to go.

"How are you doing?" Paul asked.

"Pretty good," replied Theo.

Two teenaged runners, a boy and a girl, passed them. "I think we could speed up some," Paul said.

Theo thought for a second. "Go ahead if you want. I'd better just stay like this for now."

Paul nodded but didn't speed up. He stayed next to his friend. The course now turned a corner into the downtown area. There were a number of people on the sidewalk, watching. Some had brought folding chairs. They cheered and applauded and yelled out encouragement to the runners going by.

"Hang in there!" "Way to go!" "Just do it!"

It felt good to hear it. Paul glanced over at Theo. "See those two who passed us a few minutes ago? Want to try to catch them?"

Theo looked to see the ones Paul meant, about fifteen yards ahead and now going at about the same pace. "Yeah, why not?"

The boys quickened their stride and soon were within ten yards of the teenagers . . . then only five. One of the two looked back over her shoulder and said something to her friend, who also looked back. The two then upped their speed and widened the gap again.

"Forget it," Theo said. "Maybe they're just faster runners. Anyway, it'd be crazy to try to keep up with them."

They picked up more to drink at another station. Theo felt sweat dripping from his face. A minute later, they passed the 2K sign.

As they did, Paul said, "Yo, Gee, check this out."

One of the kids who had sprinted away from them at the start of the race was standing off to the side of the runners. He was bent over with his hands on his knees, and he seemed totally wiped out. Theo and Paul exchanged a look. They had been right to pace themselves.

Now they had reached the slight uphill grade that Steve had mentioned. It wasn't much of a hill, but on a hot day, and after running for a while, it seemed pretty rough to Theo, whose face felt really hot now. For the first time, he felt a little doubt creep in about whether he could finish this race.

A refreshment station appeared up ahead, just where the hill leveled off. As Theo grabbed for some water, a volunteer yelled, "Pour it over your head! It'll help."

Theo did it and immediately felt cooler and better. He grabbed another cup from a volunteer and drank it down. Paul, seeing what Theo had done, poured some water over himself. "Great idea!" he yelled.

The boys passed the three-K mark. The course was now headed back toward the park. Theo wondered if his parents and Marj had made it to the park by now, but for the most part he concentrated on running. He realized that his fists were clenched and relaxed his arms and hands.

Next to him, Paul turned and said, "I want to speed up. How about you?"

Theo shook his head. "Not now. Go on, I'm okay. See you later."

Paul moved ahead, and Theo kept the same pace. Seconds later, Theo found himself in the shade of some tall buildings and began running slightly faster. Relaxing his arms and the cooling effect of the water he'd thrown on his head had made him feel a little stronger.

He saw Paul about twenty yards ahead of him as he passed the 4K sign. It wouldn't be too much longer before he'd be back in the park. Theo imagined that the really fast runners — the guys who were up there with Steve LaMotta — had probably finished the race some time ago. He ran on, hoping there was a refreshment station not far ahead. There was.

Getting a cup of sports drink from the table, Theo drank most of it before tossing the cup aside. About fifteen yards in front of him, he saw the second of the two kids who had sprinted off at the beginning of the race. The girl had slowed down a lot, and Paul had passed her. Theo wondered if he, too, could catch and pass her. He decided to give it a shot.

He picked up some speed and focused on her back as she ran. Very slowly, the distance between them shrank. Theo figured that there was about half a kilometer — a little more than a lap on the track — left to go. He sped up a bit more and now trailed her by about ten yards. He passed a couple of other runners, but concentrated on the girl. He could see the entrance to the park about a hundred yards away. The girl was now only seven or eight yards ahead of him, and there were no runners between them.

Suddenly, she looked over her shoulder and saw him gaining on her. She put on some speed and moved further ahead of Theo, catching up to Paul.

Just before the park entrance, Theo took a deep breath and quickened his pace. Paul and the girl were now even, and Theo got a little closer to them. The finish line was now less than three hundred yards away. Did he have enough time and energy to overtake them?

He could hear cheering from the crowd at the finish line. Other runners were finishing and getting applause. He was now running in shade and didn't think he could go any faster than he was going. But he was gaining on Paul and the girl. They were ten yards ahead.

With two hundred yards to go, Theo was only five yards back. He concentrated on his breathing and on narrowing the gap. It shrank to four yards and then three. There were less than a hundred yards to go.

The girl looked back again, and her eye caught Theo's. She smiled at him . . . and sped up, passing Paul. Theo realized that he'd never catch her. She had too much left.

Now Paul looked back and saw Theo only a few yards behind him. He, too, smiled. But instead of speeding up, Paul slowed down a little. Theo pulled even with Paul, who reached out a hand. Theo grabbed it and the two boys crossed the finish line together. A digital clock over the finish line said that they had run the race in twenty-seven minutes and fifty-four seconds.

A man in an official's shirt came over and led the boys into a shaded area, where both grabbed cups of water and drank them. Then they poured more water over their heads. Theo suddenly felt tired, but he also felt excited and happy. He had done it!

He heard his name being called from the noisy crowd of spectators. Paul nudged him and pointed to where some of their ballplaying buddies, including Van Sluman, were standing and cheering. Theo and Paul waved and smiled. Then Theo caught sight of his parents standing nearby, next to the Baskins. Standing beside Mrs. Gordimer was Marj. She was beaming and clapping with the others.

Paul and Theo walked over to their families, and there were hugs and handshakes all around. Mr. Baskin grabbed Theo and Paul by their shoulders.

"Congratulations, guys. Well done."

After hugging each of his parents, Theo came up to Marj. They stood there, smiling at each other.

"Well done, young man," she said. "You make me proud."

Theo said, "I didn't exactly win."

"Sure you did. You won big-time."

Theo said, "Well, *you're* the one who won the big fight."

Marj laughed. "Then we're *both* winners." She noticed Paul standing nearby, smiling at her.

"Correction," she said. "We're *all* winners."

Theo understood that Marj was absolutely right.

Matt Christopher

Sports Bio Bookshelf

Kobe Bryant

Terrell Davis

John Elway

Julie Foudy

Jeff Gordon

Wayne Gretzky

Ken Griffey Jr.

Mia Hamm

Tony Hawk

Grant Hill

Derek Jeter

Randy Johnson

Michael Jordan

Lisa Leslie

Tara Lipinski

Mark McGwire

Greg Maddux

Hakeem Olajuwon

Alex Rodriguez

Briana Scurry

Sammy Sosa

Tiger Woods

Steve Young

Read them all!

- Baseball Pals
- Baseball Turnaround
- The Basket Counts
- Catch That Pass!
- Catcher with a Glass Arm
- Center Court Sting
- Challenge at Second Base
- The Comeback Challenge
- Cool as Ice
- The Counterfeit Tackle
- Crackerjack Halfback
- The Diamond Champs
- Dirt Bike Racer
- Dirt Bike Runaway
- Double Play at Short
- Face-Off
- Football Fugitive
- Football Nightmare
- The Fox Steals Home
- The Great Quarterback Switch
- The Hockey Machine
- Ice Magic
- Inline Skater
- Johnny Long Legs
- The Kid Who Only Hit Homers
- Long-Arm Quarterback
- Long Shot for Paul
- Look Who's Playing First Base
- Miracle at the Plate
- Mountain Bike Mania

- No Arm in Left Field
- Olympic Dream
- Penalty Shot
- Pressure Play
- Prime-Time Pitcher
- Red-Hot Hightops
- The Reluctant Pitcher
- Return of the Home Run Kid
- Roller Hockey Radicals
- Run, Billy, Run
- Run for It
- Shoot for the Hoop
- Shortstop from Tokyo
- Skateboard Renegade
- Skateboard Tough
- Snowboard Maverick
- Snowboard Showdown
- Soccer Duel
- Soccer Halfback
- Soccer Scoop
- Spike It!
- The Submarine Pitch
- Supercharged Infield
- The Team That Couldn't Lose
- Tennis Ace
- Tight End
- Too Hot to Handle
- Top Wing
- Touchdown for Tommy
- Tough to Tackle
- Wheel Wizards
- Windmill Windup
- Wingman on Ice
- The Year Mom Won the Pennant

All available in paperback from Little, Brown and Company